God Is an Atheist

God Is an Atheist

a novella for those who
have run out of time

N. Nosirrah

illustrations by A. Nosirrah

SENTIENT PUBLICATIONS

First Sentient Publications edition 2008
Copyright © 2008 by Tragic Circumstances, LLC

A paperback original

Cover design by Kim Johansen
Book design by Adam Schnitzmeier
Illustrations by A. Nosirrah

Library of Congress Cataloging-in-Publication Data

Nosirrah, N.
  God is an atheist : a novella for those who have run out of time
/ by N. Nosirrah. -- 1st Sentient Publications ed.
     p. cm.
  ISBN 978-1-59181-072-8 (pbk.)
  I. Title.

PS3614.O7835G63 2008
813'.6--dc22

                              2008000724

Printed in the United States of America

10 9 8 7 6 5 4 3 2 1

SENTIENT PUBLICATIONS
A Limited Liability Company
1113 Spruce Street
Boulder, CO 80302
www.sentientpublications.com

Those who understand these writings have no need to meet me, those who do not understand have no reason to meet me, and those who need to meet me have no need to read my writings.

—N. Nosirrah

TO SAY THIS account is strange might give the reader a way to relate to it, but in fact, nothing will shift the burden away from the reader. In these pages, the world is bent around the reader's mind until either the mind itself begins to bend, or indeed, breaks. This is a story without plot, characters, structure, or obvious purpose—an endless descent into the netherworlds of a dystopian mind, a soul adrift, a heart not so much shattered as unhinged. If a thousand monkeys typing endlessly would eventually produce all great works of literature, then this is their first draft.

I didn't find this written on a golden tablet or by a burning bush. I didn't fast in the desert or have some kind of revelation. I am not a prophet, a mystic, seer, or anything like that. I am a marginal writer with an irritated editor who works in a publishing company that can't figure out how to go digital when the old people want books at a deep discount, but made out of paper, and the young people don't read. My best days as a writer are so far behind me that I was closer to success in my last lifetime than I am to it in the current one.

2 • God Is an Atheist

I didn't even recognize its importance when I found this scrawled on the door of a toilet stall in the Denver airport: "The religious and atheist are of the same order—believers. One believes in an idea called God, the other believes in an idea called rationality." Its importance is that it adds an element of foreshadowing to my story that will later be seen as significant, and give my writing the sense of depth and quality, or at least the ambiguity that it might have depth and quality, which will make it worthy of freshman English literature classes.

I started noticing these kinds of messages all around. I saw this graffiti on the brick wall by the post office: "The end of the age of belief is near." Here I repeat the foreshadowing just in case the earlier one was missed, and to build some tension.

But, back to the story itself.

Believers believe in their beliefs, unbelievers believe in their unbelief, and no one sees beyond the structures of belief itself. It got me thinking about the whole belief game and how we can get so caught up in the content of our belief.

It is better to believe in a compassionate God than to believe in a wrathful one. It is better to believe in Science, rather than to believe in an unprovable deity. It is better to live from Faith than to live from Mind. It is better to proceed from Scripture than to do so from Man's Laws. It is better to live from the empirical than to live from the religious.

Each of these broad belief systems that we accept then breaks down into multiple belief components. Believer One may be a Christian who believes in Christ and an inerrant Bible. Believer Two may be a Christian who believes in Christ and that the Bible is open to interpretation. These two believers no doubt consider themselves in dispute, when in fact they are in profound agreement: their agreement is that they believe at all.

All of which leads me up to an incident that I will describe as best I can, and entirely subject to my editor's mostly irrational and random acts of deletion, insertion and otherwise mucking about with my prose. Here it goes, and good luck:

I was talking to God the other night, when He told me something disturbing, and truthfully, somewhat baffling. Now, you probably doubt that I was talking to God, and likely think I was delusional, or talking to myself, and you might be right about that, but as I am trying to explain, in a way I don't care what you believe, or what I believe for that matter. I only care what God believes, and that is what is so troubling. God told me he is an atheist, he doesn't believe in himself, he doesn't believe in belief, and he thinks that all the believing that people get into has caused nothing but problems.

The conversation threw me into a paroxysm of paradox and a quandary of conundrum. I had, after all, spent a great deal of my life seeking the truth of God, the ultimate answer to the meaning of life. Now I had, more by accident than by skill, finally bumped into God himself, more or less walking down the street, and the main message for me was to stop believing, not just in God but in anything and everything. It just didn't add up. Here was God, in front of me, telling me he didn't believe in God, he didn't believe in me, He wasn't, and neither was I.

For the existentialists, the nihilists, the non-dualists, the atheists, and the secular humanists, this is probably seen as good news. For the religionists of all kinds from fundamentalists to universalists, ritualists to quietists, this may seem like a kick in the collective kneeling keister. But it is not exactly what it seems. Because as God explained it to me, if he is an atheist, then there is no God, he disappears into the mists, but so do all the anti-God beliefs. When insurgents win, they become the thing they fought to destroy; when God joins the atheists, will the club have Him, and then what will they do, what will they call themselves? An atheist who meets God is a believer who has lost his faith forever.

As He explains it, when you give up belief, you give up all belief, that includes the anti-belief, the belief of not this, and not that. Atheists are forced out of their certainty, and really there is nothing more pathetic than an uncertain atheist. Maybe there is something worse: sitting at an Atheist Alliance meeting having a serious discussion about life, with God as a member of your group. And that seems to be where this is all going. God is an atheist, atheists now have to admit that God is one of theirs, and really the whole structure of belief and anti-belief collapses into confusion. I for one am entirely confused.

I had a dream last night (I think it was a dream in any case) and in it I was reading the TMZ.com website where there was an account of Richard Dawkins and the Pope as secret lovers revealed, with photos of the two grinning in bed with their morning cappuccino, apparently listening to Puccini. They couldn't reveal to the world their illicit love, both careers ruined, and yet they couldn't live without the intense draw to the intellect and the passion of their belief and anti-belief. It was an erotic dream, I suppose, but not in the usual sense, only in the sense of the union of beliefs into something transcendent. I awoke with a start, somehow realizing how shocking and inappropriate the imagery was, Richard Dawkins wasn't the problem, but the Pope should be beyond these kinds of twists of the mind. But in that moment of waking, I saw the beauty of possibility where the two would be forced to admit in a press conference, broadcast live just about everywhere, that they really weren't sure if they had it right philosophically, that truth is pretty illusive, but that when Richard saw the Pope in the full outfit there was something so clear in the fluttering of the heart. They held hands throughout, and Richard looked radiant, which he never really did as an atheist. The Pope always looked good, but now he looked a little worried, human, even nervous, but happy in that rottweiler kind of way, still ready to go for the throat, but only if you weren't nice to Richard. The reporters pushed in for the story, but they couldn't figure out what to ask once they realized that neither of the two had any beliefs left, just each other and Puccini. I have to apologize for the account of all of this, to the affront to those who find these images insulting or worse, but I do think there is something instructive in the dream world, and in a way it prepared me to meet God.

I mentioned that I ran into God, and it was almost literally so, more like I almost ran over God. You know the feeling when you sit at a complex intersection, you try to turn right-on-red, and there is suddenly a pedestrian almost under your wheels. That was me and God. Usually the pedestrian curses you, slaps your car hood or makes a face suggesting you are a low-life undeserving of substantial insight into the nature of existence. But when I almost ran over God, he didn't do that. He also didn't look kindly at me or with forgiveness or beatifically, He didn't do anything but pause, then return to the curb so I could complete my turn without taking out the Creator of the universe. I figured this guy was different, although I didn't realize how different, of course, so I pulled over and jumped out to apologize.

Now you can apologize to your wife or husband, you can apologize to the person you bump into at the post office or the caller you kept waiting on hold, but when it comes right down to it, it is just about impossible to apologize to God. I tried, but I couldn't even figure out where to start. If God is the one running the show then what's there to apologize for, it is His omnipotent hand that moves through all of reality and all of that. Plus, when it comes right down to it, if you have sinned, how do you really have the audacity to face God anyway? This is the Sinner's Paradox.

If you don't make any mistakes in life then you don't understand what all the sinners are moaning about, how they are so weak, what the big deal is about temptation. You think everyone should be good like your little spotless self. You know that you could apologize to God because you are so pure it would go easy, humble person that you are. It is just that you don't have anything major to atone for.

What you can't realize is that you are just a sinner who hasn't met up with your sin yet. You've got the murderer, the philanderer and the thief all wired up and ready to go, along with hypocrite, gossip and liar. Then you hit your sin, your mistake, the moment that you can't get back to and change, the history that will haunt you the rest of your life, and you are a sinner, and now you know what it is all about. You realize what a fool you have been. The feigned humbleness of your life before the sin was just an idea of how to be holy and pure. You are a sinner, and so fallen, so far down, that you know that you are not worthy of taking a moment of God's time to apologize, let alone having the gall to expect forgiveness.

To ask for redemption is just not in the purview of the real and undeserving sinner. The pure need sin to find humility; the sinner needs redemption to rediscover purity, that is the Sinner's Paradox.

And here I was on the sidewalk, trying to find some words for God, who didn't even look like He needed to be placated.

God seemed to find my brain freeze amusing, and I can only speculate that there was an imperceptible shift from cosmic equanimity to what? Not curiosity, not really relish, maybe something like anthropological interest with a touch of bottomless compassion. Whatever it was that moved in the cosmos, it resulted in God and me walking to the nearby coffee shop for some direct talk, some mano a mano philosophical grappling with what the universe is all about.

You probably are wondering how I knew it was God, an important plot point and the kind of thing that skilled editors point out to their hoped-to-be best-selling authors. But since you are not my editor and I am not a hoped-to-be anything, and certainly not best-selling with a story like this, let me get to the point directly. In a novel, you have knowledge of elements of the tale because of something that occurs before in the story. There are important parts of the narrative dropped in skillfully by the writer so that the reader instinctively moves with the protagonist as he realizes something.

You probably are wondering how I knew it was God.

But, in life, you know something because you do. It is non-verifiable. It is the feeling that goes with the thought, the emotive holism that envelopes the fragment of knowledge that is the Aha! It is the ipso facto on which we build our whole reality, and we assume that this knowing is somehow agreed upon by each other of our brethren on the planet. On reflection, we can see that it is not. Our knowing is as singular and unrelated to each other's knowing as the occurrence of the writing of this sentence is to the occurrence of your reading it.

How would you know it was God if you met Him? You have no real image of God other than the religious icons, the movie actors with booming voices, the New Yorker cartoons. You wouldn't recognize God by the long white beard or robes or any of the other hackneyed images. God doesn't wear a special uniform like the priests, and He is not one of us, despite what Joan Osborne says. He doesn't have to be pious, devotional, sincere, or even loving, since there isn't any cosmic deal to cut for salvation. You would recognize God only if you weren't looking for God, or more precisely, if you were not looking from the idea of God that you have imagined, surveying the world for a match to your ideas. How do you recognize the God that doesn't fit your expectations, how do you see something that you didn't already know to look for? Are you even looking for God, or is an iPhone close enough?

But, I am digressing from the real story here, which is not the philosophical conundrum of knowing anything at all, let alone knowing God, but is just the simple occurrence of bumping into God. That is the interesting thing, not the who, what, why, when, and how, but the thing itself. We can leave the explanations to the journalists and scientists, and stay with the narrative just as it occurred. This is magical existentialism, replacing no exit with an exit that opens onto an entrance, a world of all exits and entrances, no content, no history, no explanation, just the decay of what is as the introduction of what is next. When you meet God you meet God, there is nothing to verify it, nothing that caused it, and certainly no explanation. Sorry, religionist, God is not what you thought. And sorry, atheists, it is not nothing. God is something—really something.

I wouldn't say that God is a rambler, but when he gets on a roll, he really goes, and you do get the sense that time really doesn't mean anything at all to him. He was pretty fired up about the believers pursuing him over the past thousands of years, and it wasn't that it was bugging him, nothing does seem to really put him out, but He did seem to be slightly baffled by the attention. Belief, from his perspective, doesn't have anything to do with what He is about, so why would believers even be interested in him? But they relentlessly chase after him, trying to get him for their own, like Nike looking for a new sports star to brand their latest sneakers. Maybe He needs a new manager.

My editor wants me to capitalize all the pronouns referencing God, He not he, Him not him, but I am going to ignore her most of the time. My editor would probably also tell me at this point that I am going to lose my readers, I am not putting enough detail into the God character, and the story needs dialog. But, you have to understand that you don't converse with God like that, it isn't a dialectical process, not a Q and A or anything like Neil Walsh would have you believe. That would sell better, and in my reveries I have imagined the version that my editor and the book buying public would want.

"How are You, God?"

"Pretty good, how about you?"

"Okay, but something has been bothering me my whole life, and I wonder if You can help me. What is the truth?

"The truth? I don't think you are ready for it."

"I have spent my whole life preparing for meeting You, for asking the deepest question I could speak, which is about truth, absolute truth. What is the truth?"

"You are not going to like it, but the truth is your penis is too small."

"What? That's the truth? That can't be right, I don't mean my penis size, but that can't be what the truth is."

"You're right, but I like to bring that up, no pun intended, because a lot of my income depends on men having that idea. The latest survey I read had it that 55% of men believed that their male members were too small even though most women say they really don't care about penis size as long as the men bathe occasionally and talk to them intelligently. That is my work, I created that, I had to, otherwise I couldn't fund my whole operation."

"What in God's name are You talking about? What funds? What operation?"

"It's not cheap being God, talk about entourage issues, security issues, staffing the branch offices and all of that. I have a huge overhead."

"Don't the churches, the temples, the mosques take care of that?"

"You don't get it. Those are the Believers. I don't want anything to do with that money. I won't touch it, it's the only way I can stay free to be Me, you can't be God without artistic and creative freedom. Anyway they spend most of their money on marketing and building projects, as if that had something to do with Me."

"So, how do You get your money?"

"That's what I am trying to tell you, but you're not listening because you have to pretend you're a big dick, because deep down you know that your penis *is* too small."

"Okay, I'll listen but, uh, do you think you could do something for me in that size area—you *are* God after all."

"Exactly. Penis extenders. That's how I fund my operation. Penis extenders, pumps, other appliances to make your otherwise too small penis into something of colossal dimensions. I send out over thirty million discrete emails a day, you wouldn't believe the business I do. It's the answer to the prayers of the vast majority of men."

"You! You are the one flooding my email inbox. I don't believe it. That is the most bizarre thing I have ever heard. You're telling me that first You convince men that they're too small where it counts and then You provide appliances to fix it. Why do the women get let off of this scam?"

"They don't."

"You mean…"

"Right, weight loss products. Even better than penis extenders. If I weren't so busy being God I could make a fortune just reinvesting the profits. Do you have any idea what the markup on these products is?"

I fell silent, the kind of profound black hole silence in which there is no description that can escape its gravitational pull. There were so many questions I wanted to ask God at that point—like did those devices and ointments work? I suppose the real question was would they work on me. And maybe He could tell me why His spam always sounded like it came from an ESL training course with bad grammar and misspelled words, but that was probably well researched marketing.

Just hours before I had gotten God's invitation by email, written so touchingly, so directly to the heart of the male psyche that it had seared itself in my memory with its redemptive promise. Titled, "Such a big size that she never felt before," it went like this:

> Dear Customer
>
> Attention: new unequalled preparation will enlarge your phallus.
>
> It obtained popularity over the whole world and aided to many people-This is the MegaDik
>
> More than 80 000 men in the entire world have already been pleased by the quantity and efficacy of Mega Dik
>
> And this is a opportunity for you! Join to them.

I knew now that this, like all things in life, was a direct invitation from God, and a promise that faith upon Him and His works would lengthen my days and strengthen my seed, or something in that general direction. I wished I had paid more attention in Sunday school, or been raised Catholic where they didn't care if you paid attention as long as you showed up regularly, or been a Jew where you were just chosen by being born, but maybe gladly not Muslim with all the memorizing. I am not too clear what kids who are Hindu or Buddhist do on Sundays, or whether they follow the Chinese calendar in Asia like they do in Chinese restaurants and you just know that it is the Year of the Pig and leave it at that, but I guess there aren't too many Hindus in China so that can't be right.

I wish I had paid more attention in Social Studies class and in Sunday school and responded to the invitation from God for a Mega Dik.

My Mega Dik reverie was interrupted by God, apparently I had gotten it all wrong, and while God is the creator, and so all things are, in fact, a message from God for those who have faith, and all of that, the Mega Dik spam was not that kind of message or that kind of promise, it was just a funding tool, the products didn't work and almost all men had adequate penis size, including my own, I am very happy to report, especially to young and attractive female readers who might find important contemporary writers of special interest and surprisingly accessible and fascinated with those young female ideas.

This brings me to an important point, actually several points.

One is that generally men are biologically attracted to young women because they are reproductive and healthier, hence more of the man's genetic material will be passed along in the resulting children, and of course, the more young women a man has the better for the same reasons. Women are biologically looking for protection for their offspring, so powerful and large men are what is exciting. It looks like we are wired for polygamy where there are a few powerful guys with lots of lovely, reproductive ladies. This leaves a lot of pissed off men, of course, who are discarded by the biological process, and they then go off to war and kill each other, become suicide bombers or sell real estate.

The second point is, since the pen is mightier than the sword, I would like to make it clear that male writers are, therefore, the most powerful men and should be first in line in the reproductive lottery.

Those two points, while important, are my points, not God's, by the way, and this illustrates a kind of meta-point, which is that God isn't interested in making points, isn't interested in all the distinctions that we love to embroil ourselves in. (That preposition-ending sentence is left in despite the objection of my editor, who still thinks that writing is a formal expression that requires rules, while many important contemporary writers agree that if it conveys meaning it is close enough, and contemporary readers are practically illiterate anyway.) God seems to be into synthesis, holism, unitarianism, non-duality, and all of that, while the human mind seems only interested in distinctions, data points, the separation of this from that.

God's point is I AM and this doesn't leave a lot of room for distinctions, really doesn't suggest a need for theology, but that's where we come in ready to form tax exempt religious organizations and endlessly split those over theological disputes. I AM takes all the forms of reality, but we try to sort it all out, make some sense of it, and once claiming to know it, begin teaching it to others. I AM, the essential beingness even takes the form of the observing self, the endless loop of subject chasing object in the rabid search for the beingness that it already is and that's the cosmic joke that I really wanted God to explain. Not so much how it is, or even why it is, but maybe, what's the point of structuring reality like that? The real joke was that so far all we had been talking about was penis size.

I don't know if I was losing my capacity to stay in the dialog with the deity, or the double espresso was kicking in, but in the midst of the so-called conversation about reality, and what's the point of the setup and all of that, God disappeared. Actually, God didn't disappear, I disappeared and the result of that was that God did too, and the result of that was I was God, or more like unGod since it really had nothing to do with what I thought God was or how it might feel to be God or anything remotely related to the God of any religion I had ever heard about. Omniscience is not all it's cracked up to be, you really have to learn to tune out all the supplicants and their cloying prayers, there are football teams praying for a win, suicide bombers praying for virgins, little old ladies going for world peace, it goes on and on, but that's just a little static in the big picture, because the big picture is pretty large, and the thing is it isn't really made up of things, not even little things like atoms or quarks, it is made up of manifestation. Omniscience isn't knowing everything, like some kind of GodGoogle™, it is creating everything. Creating and knowing and being are enfolded, which goes to the point of prayer, which is not that useful as a supplication, which is more or less like trying to get customer service from one of the airlines.

The double espresso was kicking in.

In the Godhead things don't look different, they are the same, but just not imbedded in a movie, no plot, character development or denouement, everything just is, and isn't. The isness and isn'tness are coincidental, cocreative, codependent form and space.

What is emerges from what is not, just as what is not falls away from what is. I felt sure that I had finally seen the essence, the truth. I was wrong of course, which I realized as I crashed back into me and out of God or wherever I was, and thankfully so, because this would be a very short book, and not all that interesting, if I had gotten the truth so quickly. But what I did get was a good look at the Garden of Eden, the place of endless creation without time or division. I certainly would have gone for Eve, but I went for the apple first. I went for "I know." It was the descent into knowledge, the narrative of surety, the construction of a universe where there had just been beingness. I am becomes I know. Godhead becomes God desire. Omniscience becomes belief. What is becomes what was, what is next becomes what I want and therefore cannot have, and the whole of maya spits out into its endless worlds within worlds, all spinning so fast that the vaporous seems substantial.

As I thudded back, God again seemed amused, but maybe that was just my projection, my humiliation at my failure to reside in something other than my pathos, and the groveling search for the very transcendence I had just discovered that I could not sustain. Back seemed like death or the impending descent into a hell world, a Stage IV cancer invading my existentialist angst with the inevitable news that it was all over. This would be my last Christmas, my last birthday, my last anniversary. And when I opened the cards from my friends, "Happy Holidays," I knew they would not be so happy, or the birthday card, "You're not getting old, you're just getting better…. On second thought, you *are* getting old," with the funny picture of the old, wizened character with no teeth, and everyone laughs because no one knows that you are dying, Stage IV, where no one ever recovers.

You <u>are</u> getting old.

There are no cards for such an occasion, there is Hallmark with the maudlin messages, but there are no "Tragic Circumstances" cards for that last birthday before your terminal illness terminates you. There is no card that says "I know you are dying….I am sorry about that, but not as sorry as I would be if I was the one dying," maybe with a funny picture of a weird dog or a cat, they always make people laugh. Or a Holiday card with a gift certificate to Barnes and Noble that expires in three months since "you only have a few weeks to live anyway." Or gifts especially for those who are about gone, novellas instead of novels, or better, short stories, so your loved one doesn't go out in the middle of an unfinished story. You could launch the business by issuing short term notes.

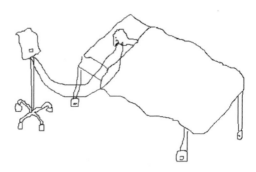

I know you are dying…I am sorry about that, but not as sorry as I would be if I was the one dying.

It occurred to me that Tragic Circumstances could be a subsidiary of the much larger 100 Is the New 30™, a company dedicated to life extension on a mass scale. Remember that the life expectancy in ancient times was 28, and in the 19th century the developed world reached 37 as the typical time to die, and you can see why 30-year mortgages didn't really develop until modern times. Now we can expect about 75 years in the United States, which isn't too bad, other than the Social Security system can't really handle the increasing capacity to live. Russia solved this with alcoholism; men can expect to live to be 59 there, just short of retirement. That saves a huge amount on government benefits and sells a lot of vodka, which is a big employment boost for the country.

But back to the main point which is 100 I.T.N. 30. The company guarantees it will add an average of 7 years to the life of its customers without exercise, supplements or medical treatments. It would be the first true life insurance company and time share company rolled into one, revolutionizing the life extension industry just as the Segway transporter promised to fundamentally alter our transportation systems. It will cost the customer a substantial amount, well worth it in the elegant simplicity of the plan. Basically, it will relocate each expected-to-live-until-75 American client to Switzerland where the life expectancy is 82: net increase, 7 years. I was thinking about using Japan as the destination since it has a slightly higher life expectancy, but who really wants to learn Japanese, and all the Swiss speak English so you can just pretend you are trying to learn Swiss or whatever it is they speak there.

Now I was out of my funk and back in action, the idea of a business based on gifts and greeting cards for the soon to be deceased plus life extension for the survivors had my juices going again. It was a world within a world, it was delusional, but it was mine. I was content. Then God laughed, or at least I think He did. I snapped out of my reverie and the haze of my world cleared just enough that I could see that the world I had created, even if it was located in Switzerland, and even if I cheated death by seven years, was still a tragic circumstance because the vapors still seemed real, and my guess is that if I got a card near the end it would be a happy card, a meaningful card, a poetic card from someone trying to make me feel good. It wouldn't be an honest card. It wouldn't say, "You are not dying, because you were never born." When the vapors clear, you can call that death I suppose, if you are referring to the mists of mind, but if you are looking through all of that, and see the wide openness of the space in which those bits of mist occur, you wouldn't say anything is happening at all. Nothing is born, nothing dies.

I meant to ask God about the story of Jesus and his followers, where they saw that he could raise the dead, and pestered him for the secret Word that was the key to resurrecting those who had passed over. Was this a metaphor, a teaching story about something else, power, hubris, but not really about death? Passing over, passing back, from where to where? In the story, Jesus for some reason gives in to the followers who insist they are ready to handle the good stuff, to use it only as instructed, and he gives them the secret Word that will raise the dead. The followers are cruising around in the desert at some later time, see a pile of bones, can't resist trying out the new power, and bring the bones back to life. Well, it's the bones of a ferocious beast that leaps at them and eats them up, end of story. It is probably about the misuse of power, but I could have gotten the real interpretation from God if I had thought of it.

Then there is the story about the man in Baghdad who hears that Death is going to be busy collecting souls in the city (and this is an old Sufi story, but not much different than today in Baghdad it would appear). To escape the touch of Death, the smart guy takes off for Samarkand, which is a two week camel ride from Baghdad. Meanwhile, Death is surprised to find that the guy was even in Baghdad, because in Death's appointment book he has a meeting with him in two weeks…in Samarkand.

That story seems pretty clear, with Death, when your time is up, your time is up, but God told me when He first told it to Fudail ibn Ayad it wasn't really about Death per se, it was more about how we live.

We can't escape from where we are, even though we spend a great deal of our life trying to improve what we are, to reconcile what we have been and to become what we are not. What we escape to is what we were trying to escape from and there is no way to game the system, other than possibly to relax and enjoy the camel ride.

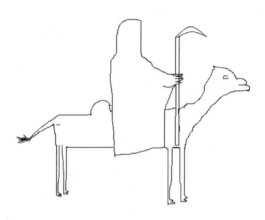

When your time is up, your time is up.

Fudail ibn Ayad, who told the story of the appointment with Death to his students in the 9th century, had one thing going for him. When God spoke, he actually listened.

Fudail ibn Ayad was a robber and people were ter-
rified of him as a result. But when God spoke to him,
he listened, not the following week, or at a convenient
time, but right then and there, which happened to be
as he was climbing the wall around the house of a
woman with whom he had fallen madly in love. He
stopped being a robber on the spot, repented, never
even made it over the wall, so the woman was never
mentioned again and after people got over being terri-
fied of him because of his past they recognized a real
mystic and a great storyteller.

That's what God told me, and apparently it is unusual that people actually listen, even though God
says He is talking all the time. I realized that one of
the benefits of listening to God is that your stories
are remembered at least for the next 12 centuries, and
presuming that Disney continues to be successful at
extending the copyright periods for Mickey Mouse
and all other intellectual property, that could make
my heirs in the year 3208 pretty happy, assuming 12%
royalties on net sales, dollar cost averaged into a good
index fund.

I was listening very hard to God. Maybe that's
what J.K. Rowling did, too, but it's hard to listen to
God and calculate compounded royalty rates at the
same time. I think that was the point God was trying
to make—that very few people can actually listen. We
can't listen to our friends, our kids, or spouses. We
can't listen to the birds, the wind or the water rushing

in the creek. We can't listen to our bodies, our dreams or our own feelings. How are we going to listen to God?

God speaks in the softest of tones and the harshest of manners. As the all and everything of the universe, He speaks in every form. That's the rub. If He would just show up Hollywood style, speak in a Charlton Heston voice, we would find it easy to listen. But He shows up as the constant flow of life itself, in every piece, every quality, in the whole range from ecstasy to calamity. We generally only listen to the part we like, and don't want to hear the part we don't like. We start to form God's voice as the part, rather than the whole, and that's where we form our belief, collect others who agree, and look slightly askance at those who don't. God is still talking as the everything, it is just that we are only listening to the something. Nobody is going to remember our stories about something, what endures is the everything.

That is why the age of belief is over, it can't sustain itself, because belief is always the belief in just a piece of the everything. God's voice, the voice of everything, is all that really endures.

And yet, here I was going on in my explanation of how it all is, and God is there, and I am not listening to God, just to my own babble. We want to listen to God, but we just don't have the ability. More accurately, it is lack of interest. Our real interest lies intractably in our selves. We go through the motions of listening to

God but we are really just waiting for a chance to lay out our complaints.

I really had to ask God what I should do. It all seemed so confusing. If I could just know God's plan for me, I felt sure I would be content. I had recently sent money to a televangelist who said he knew God's plan for my life, but apparently the plan was that I continue to send money to the preacher's organization. I wrote back saying that God had spoken to me very directly and that the preacher was supposed to send *me* money, but I never got a cent. The preacher did put me on his mailing list, which started out with fairly benign appeals to support him, but later degenerated into threats of eternal damnation if I didn't capitulate and send money. I thought about it. Maybe he was right and it would be a cheap insurance policy for the hereafter to send him twenty-five dollars. If it is a truly mysterious universe, it is possible that it is organized around sending monetary donors to Heaven and sending the rest to burn in Hell.

Fortunately, I met God in the midst of this dilemma so I could resolve the question once and for all.

God thought the whole notion of donation for Heaven was a bit overwrought, and highly unlikely, but even God couldn't rule out a universe that worked on such bizarre principles. It turns out there are lots of universes, actually unaccountably lots, and it is hard to keep them all straight.

This may seem strange, multiple universes I mean,

not me talking with God, but those respectable quantum physicists seem to agree with God, at least on the possibility of a multiverse. Now you probably feel better about the concept, hearing that scientists think that uncountable universes could be scientific. If a physicist says it, then it is rational and not wacky. But if God says it, or worse, *I* say that God said it, then it is suddenly all blurred out in some kind of mystical realm or just plain weird.

Try this: God made the physicists, who agree that God could be right that there is an uncountable multiverse, and these God-made scientists agree that this hypothesis is scientific, although the major component of it is uncountable and therefore a bit unverifiable. These same physicists don't agree that there is a God because that wouldn't be science, even though I am sitting talking to God and there is only one very countable God and he is as scientific as he wants to be, or not, and it really doesn't bother him because he doesn't have any grants to lose or reputation to defend.

It doesn't seem to offend Him that religionists attack the multiverse by suggesting that a God-created single universe is a simpler and more plausible explanation, that the world is tuned precisely to support life and that evolution may not explain the complexity of those life forms. Nor does it bother Him that atheists ignore all of those issues. The religionists don't want to admit that God, if he wants to, can do anything he damn well pleases in as many scientifically rational universes as he wants. The atheists don't want to admit that either, of course.

The way God explains the multiverse has to do with our organization of time, well, actually to do with the fact that we don't organize time correctly. We say something happened first that caused something to happen second and if we do it again it will cause that something to happen again. This is past, present and future. Our language, our reality, our sense of self is all organized around these time elements.

God explained it very clearly and I will probably muddle it, not just because I might have missed a few key points, but also because language structures always suggest time structures that exist in the language, but nowhere else. Basically, the future defines the past, which is why there are multiple universes created by the various futures. The future pulls the past inextricably towards itself in such a way that you might get the idea that we are looking in the wrong direction when we look at what's going on. We look to the past to understand what's next when we might be looking at what's next to see how the past is being created. Weird isn't it, but time can go the other way. According to God, there is no time per se, or at least He didn't create time, we did that. We thought it up. We sliced and diced the universe into manageable pieces, and we organized them through narrative into a more or less coherent reality.

Here is what we created: Past, present, future, flowing in that direction, irreversibly so, and in a singular universe that is real, material and inhabited by me and you, also real. We agreed that anything that is beyond that reality is God. There is God and there is the material world. We decided that our job is to live in the material world, but ultimately to transcend it and realize our connection to God. Once we got that all set up and agreed that the world was like that, then we got down to the real business of fighting each other over our control of resources in the material world and our beliefs about God.

The physicists will happily suggest that time and space are not what they appear to be in our normal range of perception. Particles don't really locate without an observer, they don't really individuate when separated, and they go zinging around without causality doing the choosing. Don't worry, say the science guys, it's only on the very small level of life that there is no time, location or causality. But on the macro level where it is really important, all these Newtonian elements are obviously occurring, so we can figure out what feet to put our shoes on to get to work on time in order to keep the bills paid. Oh, really now, are we expected to believe *that*, but not believe in God? I think I will believe in the scientists and Intelligent Design and Santa Claus. Why not just have a spreadsheet of possible beliefs and randomly pick out four or five each week to believe?

But the really far out physicists agree that there is something pretty strange going on, and believe it or not, they do see that the slight observation of particle behavior actually changes what came *before* the measurement. Now are they looking forward or backward in time? Or is God right, and time is just the creation of the viewer looking, the narrative that comes from that, and the social construct around it?

God said He tried to explain all of this to a German guy on a park bench, it wasn't Meister Eckhart but it was Eckhart something, but as soon as God started explaining the German guy ran away shouting, "I got it! It's all now! And it's power!" God thought he missed the point by quite a bit, it really wasn't about "now," but of course, once it got onto Oprah there was a lot of power.

God has nothing to do with any now, and that is the whole point. Now is an orientation, but in timelessness there is no orientation and, anyway, what are you going to do with power without time? That's the real secret, and, yes, God did try to explain it to that filmmaker lady too, but she got right on the phone to share that "secret" with Oprah, too, without letting God finish his sentence. I thought God should just talk directly to Oprah, but he said her people never returned his calls. He told me he would make sure that Oprah got my book, and he was sure that after reading it she would personally invite me to be on her program, but he wanted me to be very clear that the conversation was to be a private one between me and Oprah, not me and 10 million viewers. I cannot go on the Oprah show, that's God's will and as proof of God's miraculous power you, the reader, can see that Nosirrah has never been on Oprah no matter how hard her producers have tried, no matter what the compensatory offer, no matter the resulting Amazon rating. Apparently Oprah will do fine without this book on her show, and that's certainly no secret.

I mention Oprah, not in the hopes that she will notice my mention of her and thereby notice me (I trust God will make it as He wishes in that regard), but rather because my writing teacher at Columbia, Professor Daniel Felsenfeld, used to insist that all written elements be anchored in some reality the reader could identify with, and that this ongoing chain of elements was what made coherence. He prattled on about this but no one was really listening, certainly not me, possibly because he himself was not anchored in any reality whatsoever. That was the University of Missouri at Columbia, by the way, which made the non-reality of Professor Felsenfeld even more obscure. But, occasionally I experiment with anchoring elements, which I find, at least in my writings, has the effect of breaking up the total incoherence in what I am expressing. This gives the faint suggestion of a gauzy meaning, which apparently excites the occasional reader.

Anchoring is what cognitive experts say we do all the time with the whooshing overload of reality

that is like a demon riptide bent on taking us under.
Anchoring is the recognizable element around which

My writing teacher at Columbia, Professor Daniel Felsenfeld.

we build our narrative. It is part memory and therefore the recognition of something known in what we
are experiencing, and it is the bending of all other

elements into a fit with that known. From a survival standpoint we couldn't be exploring every sensory input from a naïve perspective, we have to analyze and summarize pretty quickly and take an action. If it walks like a duck, and quacks like a duck it is probably a duck, and that is close enough to grab it, roast it and call it another day survived.

But anchoring distorts our perception because while we are surviving we are also overemphasizing our anchors as we summarize a more and more complex life into a fixed set of ideas until the whole world starts looking like ducks. Even the tigers.

Until the moment we are surprised to be gobbled up by a tiger (that we were sure was a duck), we have the ship of fools paradise of our narrative, held firmly in place by our anchors, those heavy hooks dug deeply into the mud of our minds. The problem with relying on anchors, besides getting eaten, is we don't know very much about the actual world. We just know a great deal about what we know.

Not knowing is a lot harder. No anchor. Only a kind of faith, but even that is an anchor and must be let go to discover what life is. Anchors aweigh.

Mother Teresa's posthumously published letters show that she spent the last fifty years of her life not really knowing if what she believed connected to anything at all, and she had to function on the faint fumes of her faith. She had to be saintly because she was more or less considered a saint, but she had lost her mystic connection to Jesus and shared with her confessors a wrenching disconnection from her own source of direction.

Now you can look at it that she was a hypocrite for acting like nothing was the matter at all and proceeding to minister to the sick and dying as if she was in communion with her God. Or you can see this as a test of faith so deep and dark that few would pass through without renunciation of their beliefs. What would you do if Jesus gives you a call one day, tells you to drop everything and take a whole new direction in your life and then hangs up the phone and just doesn't call back again. Ever. And there you are, not knowing. That's what happened to Mother Teresa.

Faith can fill in, but as Mother Teresa found out, faith has to be destroyed in order to live in not knowing. Faith as it turns out is not the access to the mystical, but the barrier. Not knowing is not *just* not knowing what Jesus wants, but not knowing if Jesus ever even called. Not knowing anything with certainty, and still living fully. Did Mother Teresa live fully in the not knowing? We don't know, and likely she didn't know either.

When I asked God about faith and Mother Teresa, he couldn't place the name, but said he could google her and get back to me with what actually happened there. But, I suppose that proves her point, God didn't know anything about her. Her sainthood was generated on her abandonment by the object of her worship.

That should be lesson to all of us who are aspiring to be saints, or even trying to be faithful. It isn't really that easy to even know what it means to be faithful, especially if it means that we have to give up our faith first and then see what is left, if anything. Perhaps what is left is something we know nothing about. No anchor.

I was curious about the fact that God did not seem to even recognize one of the most famous saintly figures in our times, and so I had to ask him who he thought was doing a good job as a human being. He started listing off names and addresses of people like He was reeling off a memorized phone book, which I soon realized was exactly what he was doing. I couldn't quite get the point at first, it seemed that either there were a lot of hidden saints or pretty much everybody was doing well in the faith and practice department. But then I got what he was talking about.

From God's vantage everyone is doing exactly as well as they can, each one is on the edge of their capacity, and no one is standing outside of that capacity deciding whether to use it or not. In other words, there is no moral decider, there are just decisions, which one could reflect on as moral or not. None of us are deciders, there are just decisions. No actors, just actions. Everyone is at their peak sainthood for their capacity at all times, because where else could they be?

The various churches, mosques and temples have been trying to convince us for a long time that we must develop our morality. God laughs at this notion, and apparently this is one of the reasons He continues to run hard from religions of all kinds. The moral agent, apparently, is a construction, an idea cooked up by the philosophers and the theologians.

God is the decider. God assured me that He does the doing and everything else does the being, and the only moral agency resides in the individual chucking the security of morality and landing square in the Godhead where the action is. And if God told you that the Godhead is the place of interconnectedness, not a place of right and wrong, you'd more or less have to consider it, right? Wrong. I really didn't want to consider it at all, it was too wild and crazy for me. I was a good person, most of the time, and I was basically comfortable with that. I wasn't that big on religion, so I was in agreement with God there, but now to accept that right and wrong were equivalent, or actually worse, that they did not exist, sent me into a spiral of reaction.

I could see the God had a point. It was just so simple and so radical that we can't bear to accept it. We don't have free will because we are just a mess of biochemical impulses, no beginning or end, with an epiphenomenological notion of self describing back to ourselves a story of good and bad actions that, by the way, already happened without anything other than the story of a decision deciding. My head was spinning trying to find a firm place where I could stand, make a decision that was free of any prior impulse, prior conditioning, prior knowing, that was my decision, not God's decision flowing through me. The spinning didn't stop and like a Sufi whirling into the divine ecstasy I was transported to some alternate reality in which all that took place was an expression of God's will. It was a surprisingly relaxing condition to find myself in, because the burden of righteousness and sin had disappeared, the need to moderate my impulses, to select for the action that was good, to concern myself with the implications of my deeds, had vaporized. It wasn't that each movement of mine was perfect, it was just as it was, and the source of that movement was the source of all movements of life.

Even as my mind continued to spin, and even with the total freedom that I could sense with every fiber of my being, it still shocked me to the very marrow of my bones when Immanuel Kant walked in at that very moment and began shouting at me. The spinning mind stopped, the heart began pounding. I felt a defensive stance developing in my now rigid body. Kant was yelling at me, calling me a complete idiot. He claimed I was deluded, that there is a categorical imperative for true moral action, and demanded to know what would happen if everyone began acting as I was now prepared to act, free of guilt, free of fear, free of any second-guessing.

I tried to explain to him that I had no idea what would happen under these new and unexpected conditions, and that was the very point. There was an exhilarating unknown where once there had been the stultifying weight of the morass of moralizing. I could feel the deep freedom, and with that sense of no boundaries, no limitations, no restrictions came an entirely different context and perspective. The moral action wasn't the result of good decisions made after the weighing of right and wrong, but rather it was the movement directly from this unlimited space. The moral action was the action that was whole and undivided, that had no me and you in it, that had no separation of good or bad. It was the action that was already taking place, it was a priori and therefore free of the taint of any narrative that might describe it in moralistic terms.

"But, you must act in a way that you would want all people to act," Kant screamed, red in the face, flustered and bug-eyed, "Only an imbecile could live without an examination of his actions!"

As I recalled, Kant was an advocate of free will and so it would make sense to him to universalize your actions to see if they were the right ones or not, but, nevertheless, he was getting on my nerves.

So, I punched him in the nose. Why, I have no idea, I am not really a punching kind of guy, but the fist moved, and I did punch him. For a moment the story appeared as a blip in my mind that I had wanted to punch him, but that blip unblipped and there was no narrative. I didn't universalize, moralize or second guess. Strangely, I felt no remorse. He shut up. Then he disappeared. Then I woke up.

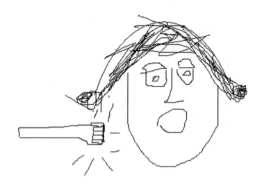

So, I punched him in the nose.

God was shaking me, saying I had passed out after spinning around and around like a ballerina on methamphetamines. Apparently they had asked us to leave the coffee shop and God had gotten me half-way down the block, me still spinning like crazy before I fell over.

If Kant comes to you in a dream, is it universally moral to punch him in the nose? If you punch Kant in the nose and there is nothing but the action, is there an actor who is good or bad? If you feel remorse after punching Kant in the nose is that better than if you feel nothing at all and then wake up? The multiverse is a confusing place at times, but there is something soothing in the fact that all the interlacing realities are far too complex to make any sense at all, so we just don't have to bother trying sometimes.

The scientists just won't give up in this regard. They relentlessly pursue an explanation that makes sense, usually settling for a description. But none of them will face the fact that they are believers of the worst kind. They believe in science, of course, that is a given. But, more fundamental than that is that they believe in an orderly universe, a lawful universe, and all of their science, all of their belief flows from that one basic belief. Who said the universe is orderly anyway? Isaac Newton started it, but he got the idea from the Catholic Church.

Does anyone see the irony of this? Scientists would not be scientists if they did not believe in a world of natural laws, but why does a universe need natural laws? Universes don't make natural laws, people make natural laws. Scientists really cannot know if the universe is an acausal, chaotic, anarchistic jumble of occurrences, what they *can* know is that they *believe* that it is *not*. They have so much faith in their belief that they are willing to spend their entire brutish and short life in the temples of their religion, the universities and laboratories. They can deride the religious believers, but this is sectarianism, not enlightenment.

All human beings, even scientists, are believers because we have faith that the universe is operating from knowable laws: natural laws, God's laws, some kind of order. But what if Newton and the Church got it wrong? What if it is a multiverse in which everything is happening without time, causation or meaning with such chaotic complexity that the little pea brains called humans are just never going to understand it? I for one am going to grab on to something, and frankly, even if I have to read Ken Wilber, I don't care, because otherwise my head might explode. As long as I don't have to go to Ken's loft—I don't think I am hip enough.

There remains this nagging question about the universe as it is, which is something like: "Why?" In the immortal words of the blues queen Jenn Cleary, "Why, oh why, can't there be peace in our world?"

Why is there suffering? Why old age? Why pain? Why Barry Manilow? Why is it set up like this? I turned to God for the answer.

God would have none of it. He was hustling me towards the Quick Stop where He was intent on acquiring some Slim Jim Beef Jerky. I am sorry to tell all of you vegans, vegetarians, Jains and animal rights folks out there, but God is an indiscriminate omnivore. By that I don't mean you should be shocked that he eats meat, but shocked because as an indiscriminate omnivore he eats vegans, vegetarians, Jains and animal rights folks. He eats everything. Actually, not vegans very often, they're too skinny. But if you think that caring for animals is going to protect you from God's appetite for consuming the universe, digesting it and spewing the remains into the vacuous nothingness as the universe that is next, you need more time in reflection and less at the PETA rally. It is not a dog eat dog world, it is a God eat dog world. And everything else, too.

God eats the universe, bizarre as that may sound. But, it gets worse, because actually *He* doesn't do it, *She* does. I swear, whether you believe me or not, that as God and I walked from the convenience store and as He chomped on the beef jerky, He became She and as She explained, these are just aspects anyway. Gender issues apparently are man's creation, and even in writing this sentence you can see how difficult it is to avoid them, because gender issues are not "man's" creation, they are really man and woman's creation. God doesn't have gender issues, he just appears as any damn shape he wants and finds it amusing that humans are so involved in identities and their forms.

But here She was chomping on the jerky and maybe it was my head still spinning from my recent fall, but if I looked closely it did seem like the whole universe was getting taken in and expelled out, in and out, like a breath, like the universe breathing but it was being digested and regurgitated. And God's form was not just changed from He to She, but also from an almost nondescript, vaguely luminous and enfolding presence to a rather threatening, dark and scary, no terrifying, form. She was wild eyed and ravenous looking, teeth as sharp as needles, tongue hanging out. She had a sort of dancing, jerky gait, and she was suddenly looking at me like I was her next meal.

I started to back away. I thought about running. I thought about making the sign of the cross or calling on Jesus, but that would be pointless when you are already dealing with God.

She laughed. Then she gobbled me up.

Then she spit me out.

Then is not really the right word because the gobbling and the spitting out were not in sequence, not in a before and after. But, I will use the imperfection of words here. The world had transformed upon the spitting out, I was the same in every possible way and yet I was completely and totally different. I knew it but I couldn't prove it. The only thing that was clearly altered was that God was back to He and He didn't look hungry at all.

Disregarding that I was in an alley by the parking lot of a convenience store in a fairly congested urban environment, I let out a scream, or maybe it was a wail, that was something like this, "What just happened??"

And God in His sublime grace attempted to explain it to me. It was pretty heady stuff, but I will try to do it justice in the hopes that this narrative will become at least slightly coherent.

Emptiness and form, stillness and movement, these are aspects of the universe at its most basic

Then she spit me out.

elemental level. God doesn't get caught up in the aspects, as I have mentioned, but we do. We love our form and our actions, we become very attached to them, and generally we forget about the fact that this is just one side of the coin. When we glimpse the other side, emptiness, stillness, we come to an insight that shows us that form and movement are only apparent, not actual.

This is such a wonderful insight that we get very enamored, and reside in that still point, watching the fools of form go about their sorry lives. But the insight that was so fresh a moment ago itself becomes a structure, the stillness becomes resistance to movement and emptiness becomes fear of form. And there we are, once again on the first side of the coin, or is it the other side?

Form becomes formless becomes form becomes formless...these are the aspects transforming. The transformer is God. And when God comes to transform, He comes as She. She comes hungry. She devours what is there and spits out what is not there. Form becomes formless becomes form becomes formless. And just as a kicker, even though this movement is constant, it is not in time at all.

What is known will become unknown, and this is why She looks so terrifying. It is our clutching to the known that makes the impending trip to the unknown so frightening.

Those who think they can stand in any place, form or formless, will meet this feminine God force, and the place that they stand will be transformed into what is next. They will be eaten and spewed out in new form

and new formlessness. There is no place that is safe
from the destruction and no place safe from the creation. God is an indiscriminate omnivore.

This all reminded me of India, where they tell the
story of Shiva, who represents the absolute stillness
of pure consciousness and who gets to that state only
after long austerities and the denial of all forms. He is
in mega-bliss, the bliss beyond bliss, staring unblink-
ing at the world that does not exist. Kali, who represents energy and movement, comes along, but she
isn't in the fanged form or looking nasty at all. She
is Shakti and she can shake it. She dances, Shiva notices, more than notices, and with a sudden squirt of
his semen the universe is created. Silence plus energy
equals reality.

In India they tell all kinds of stories, trying to
explain the order and chaos, the endless stream of life
flowing down the Ganges and the endless death of
the ashes swept into the river from the burning ghats,
fires that have been continuously burning bodies for
thousands of years. Whatever you believe will be shak-
en by India, there you will find nothing but paradox.
Even that paradox is wrapped in a paradox as India
becomes a technology center and begins outsourcing
its customer service to North Dakota and importing
American programmers to its cubicle farms.

Globalization is not just the grand mobility of
capital beyond national borders to wherever labor is
desperate enough to be cheap, it is also the battle of

belief, the market consolidation of vast concepts of reality. Free market and socialism, Muslim and Christian, Pepsi and Coke all vie with each other for market share and with emerging brands that threaten to upset an either/or consumer choice: sustainable Greens, Mormons, Dr. Pepper. But belief is still the winner, even an environmentalist Mormon drinking Dr. Pepper knows what he believes, and most importantly believes in those beliefs. The belief market knows us better than we know ourselves, and it is grinding us down into a Soylent Green of uninspected concepts, all the better to sell us by, to consume the consumers. We know how to respond to every stimulus, because we know what we believe, we have just forgotten why we believe. This is the slow descent into the undifferentiated world where kitsch and culture merge into a grand Wal-Mart shopping session and Happy Meals of the soul. We believe, we consume, we consume belief, we believe in consuming and we are consumed by our belief. God help us.

He is trying. That was what He was telling me, that He is trying to help us. But how do you get this across to people if you are God? If you appear to someone, then you have not just created a believer, but you now have a mystic, certainly a small cult, or possibly a new religion. Remember, God tried chatting with various guys in the Middle East over the past few thousand years and look what came of it. Prophets, saviors, and millions of people who have come to believe that a rather casual conversation with God was somehow important, even inerrant. Imagine if you saw someone interesting at the grocery store, and talked about your son, your work and the weather and the guy you were talking to thought it was so damn profound that he started a religion. You'd probably be hesitant to go to that grocery store again, at the very least, and you might start keeping a bit more to yourself.

On the other hand, if God ignores humankind, they really get agitated and start going apocalyptic, or messianic and that really can convert some believers. If you are God you have to work the edges, drop some hints, a little guerilla marketing, and hope your actual message spreads. It is not a new brand God wants to establish, after all, it is a whole new marketplace. Not a new version of an old belief system, but a whole new form of human consciousness.

I suppose that was why God was hanging with me, since I exist on the fringe anyway, what better place to launch some viral marketing for a human culture beyond belief? I am not going to start a religion, no one would believe me, you don't even believe me and you are one of the few people who have read this far. Many have discarded this account pages ago, most never got past the first few paragraphs, placing the book back on the shelf at the book store where it will soon be returned to the distributor who will complain to the publisher about overstock levels and the publisher will pragmatically sell off the large quantity of returns to a remainder dealer who will unload as many of them as possible to discount bins around the country before dumpstering the rest.

God doesn't have to worry about Nosirrah creating more believers. In an obvious expression of His omniscience, He chose me, someone who has no credibility at all. God chose a novelist, who will recount his meeting with God as fiction rather than as something profound. God chose me because my life hasn't gone well, I have been shredded, my books have been shredded, every bit of my meaning and purpose in life has been shredded. Even as I write this I no longer believe that I am Nosirrah the writer, even as the words flow out, suggesting that I am. You are one of a sparse few readers who might actually understand what I am saying. I know with absolute certainty that my very existence is a fiction, and that yours is too. God chose me because I do not exist, and because He does not exist, and He wants you to know that you do not exist. This is your liberation from belief, and your liberation from the God of your imagination, and your liberation from the weight of holding yourself together with the sticky glue of your ideas. That liberation is the final liberation, it doesn't even survive itself, there is no trace of any event, any experience, anything to hang some new belief on, no way to spread the good word, no way to preach or pander. It is that nothing ever happened, or will ever happen. It is the end of belief with God still standing there, but no believer to make anything out of Him. It is the end of God. But if God ends and there is no one to know that, then there is no end, and indeed there was never any beginning.

We had left the alley now for the main street, a busy jumble of shops, restaurants, and bars. I had glimpsed the transcendental and now I was thrust into Mammon. God didn't seem fazed by the sudden commercial atmosphere. Buskers juggled on unicycles, raspy voiced burn-outs strummed guitars with cases open for change, Scientologists offered free personality inventories. A street person asked God for spare change, which He readily produced, but as we walked on, God wondered out loud why none of the panhandlers asked for something more substantial. It probably never occurred to anyone to ask for large sums, you don't see signs that say "Will work for a million dollars," or "Spare thousands?" although I did see a guy with a sign that said "My arms are tired from holding this sign." It is somewhat the same principle. We ask for spare change, a meager request that is usually resented, or guiltily responded to. We define our poverty by our state of mind. Holding our state of mind takes a lot of energy. My sign could read, "My mind is tired from holding this thought."

At the same time, we are all looking for signs. Not just written words on cardboard, like the "Free Hugs" guy, that one is too easy. We look for signs that God loves us, that life is good, that we are protected, that what we are doing is the right thing. I tried this once, seriously looking for omens, concentrating on all the elements around and I was willing to respond

My mind is tired from holding this thought.

immediately and in complete surrender. But, unfortunately, the first sign I came upon was the red hexagonal one reading, "Stop." So I did.

There is the question, for those of us still looking for signs, will we obey those signs, or will we just follow the ones that fit our ideas about what the signs should say? I asked God about signs, and he says he just doesn't do it that way. He experimented with it once. He stood in the middle of Times Square with a sign that said, "I am God, any Questions?" and all that happened was he got berated by a guy with a sign that said "Jesus is the Answer," otherwise he was ignored. He said the burning bush was just a chance lightening strike and if he had something to communicate he would do it a bit more explicitly. He is saving up for a 30-second spot during the next Super Bowl.

The thing about signs is that the human mind wants them so badly that it just plain creates them, their meaning and the big narrative that makes them important. We inject meaning into anything and everything in the hopes that we will feel better about the fact that we can't possibly understand what is really going on in the vastness of the multiverse. Human intelligence is limited to the universe that created it, and it cannot find its way beyond its own limitations. Given that we are the reflection of this universe's expression and that we interpret the signs of this universe from those limitations, for the most part we just settle down to a life of quiet disputation—the search for meaning through conflict and differentiation, to stand out, to be someone. We seek celebrity. It is a silly course to take in a life where there is no possibility of even understanding what we are, where we are, why we are or even *if* we are. I was certain I had

seen the fallacy of name and fame clearly. I had convinced myself in my writing I was searching for the
sound of one hand clapping, but it was really something quite different. I saw now that it was the sound
of two hands clapping that I was really seeking—the
sound of applause, acknowledgement, respect. Now
that seemed absurd. One hand, two hands, no hands
clapping, it all seemed without relevance.

The Buddhists started the whole hand clapping
business, but apparently they got it all wrong according to God. Gautama Buddha, hereafter referred to
as G. Buddha, wasn't the enlightened one, it was his
cousin Eddie Buddha. But nobody ever talks about
Eddie, not a mention in *Tricycle* or *Shambhala Sun*, and
I will get back to why that is in a little bit.

G. Buddha had grown up as a prince, and was
shocked when he first glimpsed human suffering, seeing a sick person, an old man, a corpse and finally a
holy man who didn't seem very much bothered by the
suffering of the first three. After some quick analysis,
G. Buddha decided to renounce his worldly life and
search for the peace he observed in the sadhu.

G. Buddha, as you no doubt recall, then abandoned
his wife and young child in order to pursue his life of
renunciation. No bills, no diapers, no more arguments
with the wife about watching too much football, or
whatever it was they likely bickered about. So he left,
renounced everything, and shortly was surrounded by
the New Agers of the day who insisted he teach them,

which at first he refused to do, and then, finally, he gave in. He showed how to give up every responsibility and live a stress free life lounging around …for the benefit of all sentient beings, of course. Not surprisingly, there were lots of takers, and Buddhism took off.

G. Buddha's wife, Yasodhara, finally caught up to him, perhaps looking for back child support, and brought along his son Rahula to get his inheritance. G. Buddha, being a renunciate, likely did the old pull out the pockets to show that they are empty, and said the only thing he had to give the boy was his teachings. He promptly made the boy a monk, and turned him over to his executive assistant, Sariputta, after a brief lecture on not lying. Rahula was declared enlightened at age eighteen and nothing much was heard from him after that. G. Buddha later died of acute food poisoning. Yasodhara disappears from all accounts of the time, not being considered very interesting, but in my mind I hear her complaining about her son, Rahula, "Is it too much to ask that he could have been a doctor…or at least an accountant…"

As I mentioned, Eddie Buddha, the cousin of G. Buddha, was the truly enlightened one. He did *not* leave his wife and child and did *not* renounce the world in order to lounge around for the good of all sentient beings. Instead, when he saw the "four sights"—as the later Buddhists would call the visions of illness, old age, death, and renunciation as the way out—he went deeply into the feeling of the suffering, especially the suffering of the renunciate. Deeply touched by the pain, he went to medical school, then opened a holistic clinic to relieve the suffering of those in his community, supported his wife while she finished grad school, and drove his kids to their soccer and gymnastic practices (in a bullock cart, of course). He lived a regular life. He dealt with all the challenges without turning away, and without any explanation. While people were impressed by his commitment to the people in his area, few recognized his depth of perception.

Eddie Buddha was the truly enlightened one.

(One Chinese transvestite named Loud Sue who was traveling through did press him for some teachings, and he reluctantly responded with, "Those who know don't speak, those who speak don't know" and dozens of other cryptic lines. The visitor was scribbling the whole time in his notebook. Like an ancient Seinfeld, the writings were really about nothing, the words were just in the Way.)

But Eddie Buddha is not remembered. Relatedness leaves no trace. It acts directly, it expresses without cause, it is whole.

I wanted a life like Eddie Buddha's that was clear, straightforward, regular and unfettered by the dogma of belief. I wanted a life that was compelling, which is an interesting word, meaning undeniable, gripping, but I wanted it compelled by truth. Compelling is the force exerted from the future into the past as organized by our mind. There is nothing compelling other than what you actually express, nothing before, nothing after.

I like to tell people that I am a Buddhist, not Hinayana, not Mahayana, nor Vajrayana, but the proud and sole member of the Edyana branch of Buddhism. I am still working out the doctrine, but it is something like, "See the suffering and live the response," or maybe I can simplify it to just, "Live the response" with a heart symbol. The theology is already worked out—there is none. There are no practices, it is all showtime. So it is a pretty simple religion and if we increase as rapidly as the Mormons have been doing we might be able to head them off for world domination. I say "we" optimistically since there hasn't been a convert yet.

The idea of world domination did get me thinking about the struggle of the world's governments to deal with Islamic radicalism. Here was a movement that was pretty hard to understand, although it was clear that they were pretty pissed off at pretty much everybody.

God didn't want to talk about it. I asked him every which way, trying to get his take on the jihadists, after all they were killing in his name. No comment, changed the subject, looked away, he just wouldn't deal with it. Then he spilled it, off the record, so I can't quote him directly, but well placed sources close to God have indicated that he is concerned about provoking the Islamic radicals, afraid they are going to come after him. After all, He doesn't agree with them. It is not just that He isn't even remotely supportive of stoning people as punishment for minor crimes, keeping women under layers of veils or destroying tall buildings, but the more basic issue is that the radicals are believers. For God, the infidel is the believer, any believer, in anything, but especially in Him. The true jihad—the struggle—is with the nature of belief, that it can latch onto any wacko idea and hold tight, that it can even kill for God, as if God needs help in that area. God sees the absolute hubris in the believers who revere their beliefs above all things—even the imminent God. And that is why He doesn't want to provoke them. An Islamic radical is a radical believer, and when it comes right down to it, the believer will destroy God and himself before he will let go of his beliefs. God is concerned that if they find Him, if the radical believers find God, they will blow Him and themselves up to further their beliefs. God is an apostate and therefore marked for death.

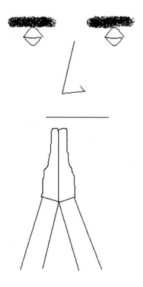

For God, the infidel is the believer.

I tried to reassure God on this point, after all they hadn't gotten Salmon Rushdie yet, and it really seemed unlikely that any mufti would issue a fatwa on God. But as I thought about it, in fact, if God was an atheist, then He was a kafir to the Muslims, for that matter He was an infidel in any religion except maybe the Unitarians—they will pretty much take anyone in. If the Unitarians start issuing fataawa then I am going to go into preemptive hiding, and so should you.

God would rather have plausible deniability in regard to the whole topic of radical fundamentalists, and for that matter so would I. God has no comment on extremists of any kind, Muslim or Unitarian, and neither do I. Anything you might have read here in this regard was inserted by my editor against my wishes. She will deny that, but don't the guilty always deny their responsibility?

This is the same editor who ruined my first book, *Practical Obsession*, which is not a shameless plug for one of the best spiritual autobiographies of all times because it is out of print anyway. They are all out of print, my legacy is in the dusty shelves of used book stores and the infinite online used books databases, not rare, just unwanted. She ruined all of my books, except perhaps *Chronic Eros*, which was, as you may have guessed, written from our bed, and she could hardly touch a word of that one, nor would she want to, proof as it is that we were once young. Yet my editor will deny her guilt in the destruction with her petty corrections—her insistent red markings on the black and white clarity I had wrestled from the pits of Hell itself—of what might have been a pristine literary career.

If there is ever success for me, it will be despite my editor, not due to her. She is like a millstone around my writing pulling it under, and me with it. But, I will not go under. I cannot stop writing my novellas until she stops editing them, and of course, she will never stop, never. We know no other way to be, and this is painful, and yet we once loved so deeply that no pain will ever erase that truth. You see, Lydia, you won't edit out that sentence will you? You know it is true. Why won't you see me? At least respond to my notes, it has been thirty years of dropping off manuscripts at an empty office, thirty years of wondering what went wrong. All right, I know what went wrong, but the trollop meant nothing then, and even less all these years later. Love is meant to be free, not just for two, no matter how intense, it is meant to be shared, even with those we encounter by chance. Lydia, you will probably cut out what is next with your red pencil because it is just too poignant, too raw, but the reader deserves to know the truth, and it will reveal the dark heart that you possess.

But, the author regrettably digresses from his meeting with God, and must return to the main story line so as not to confuse the readers who are, after all, much more interested in universal truths than the miserable failings of an aging author who is a philandering narcissist and who certainly doesn't even deserve the expert editing of his mediocre writing.

As God and I walked the main street I realized that I had been lost in reverie, once again occupied by the story of my life as it played through the endless loops of my mind. That mind came into sharp focus as I realized that unlike the rest of the inhabitants of this busy street, I was not only in the presence of God, but I *realized* I was in the presence of God. Why were they all so oblivious? Why would they walk by without noticing?

The author regrettably digresses...

If there is ever success for me, it will be despite my editor, not due to her.

God was happy to show me how it worked. He walked up to person after person, greeting them, stating clearly that He was God, asking them if they needed anything. No one could see Him. They could only see what they had expected to see, they could only see what they already knew. Their narrative filled up the space, the vastness of His being. He was seen as a madman, a beggar, a fool, an aggressor, a non-entity, a curious oddity, an invisible nobody. But no one could see Him. No one could see God because each of us is captured by what we know and we organize reality to fit it.

God then showed me something else about the human condition. He began preaching on the street corner. He made it up as he went along, the most bizarre and strange explanation of life, death, heaven and hell. People started to listen, to gather, to agree or to disagree, but to engage in the words, the meaning, the logic of what He was saying. He explained that God had appeared many thousands of years ago, leaving tablets, readable by special glasses, on top of volcanoes inhabited by clear beings from outer space who left one key representative sitting naked on an island in Fiji who would convey integral evolutionary consciousness through a special process called diksha to all those who were sincere and willing to write a good sized check and not ask too many questions. People were enthralled, or outraged, but they could see what He was describing, and whether they concurred or

opposed made no difference, it was just very comfort-
ing to have something to hold onto.

The gathering crowd grew in size and fervor. God
described to them how they should gather each week
in buildings to be purchased in key commercial dis-
tricts of urban centers around the country, where tax
free increases in value would insure financial strength.
Stand in a circle. Put the left foot in. Put the left foot
out. Put the left foot in and shake it all about. Fri-
days, Saturdays and Sundays were already taken as
holy days, there is Monday Night Football, so God
told them to grab Tuesdays as the day of worship.
Everyone had to keep their left eyebrow covered at
all times and not cut the nail on their left pinky finger
as signs of devotion. There was a lot more detail on
the rituals, of course, but you get the flavor of the
preaching.

What was amazing was that a new religion was
born on the spot and the gathering dispersed as people went off to convert or conquer, inflamed with the
fire of truth.

God sighed.

But He had another thing to show me. He began
to approach people on the street with a simple and
direct message. He proclaimed each one he met to be
God, as in, "You are God." Not "I think you are wonderful," or "You sure are beautiful and I am really attracted to you," or "You seem really deep." Not that

at all. It was, "You are God. You are it. You are the all and everything. You are Love itself, Compassion itself, Wisdom itself, all of Time and Space and everything that is not Time and Space."

Each person who received the message from God interpreted it a little differently. For the most part, it was received as just plain wrong.

No way. I am not God. I don't want to be God. I don't want the responsibility for Darfur, for George Bush, for the falling dollar, for lead in all the plastics coming from China, for global warming, for record credit card debt, subprime loans, and all the rest. It's a mess and if I am God then it is *my* mess. It is better that you be God, I will pray to you to fix it all up, and I can go about my business of surviving, reproducing and consuming.

As God continued to deliver His message to people walking down the street, occasionally someone would really take to the idea. No kidding? I am God? No way, really? You mean I can make the girls really go for me? What about the stock market, can I make it go up and down? Really. Hey I like this idea a lot.

There were a few who *really* got into it. Me? God? OK, then get down on your knees and start worshiping. I am going to start dictating a few new rules, so better get a pen and paper out.

One poor guy just simply got it. He got it completely. He got that he was God and he just popped. It is a little hard to describe but it was something like a balloon that gets overfilled and then, Blam! No more balloon.

Man. Man realizes he is God. Man pops. No man, just God.

God had a few more demonstrations.

Atheists. Now that was strange to watch. God would walk up to an atheist, introduce himself as God, and watch the atheists squirm as they explained that there was no God. He would patiently explain that while he agreed with them in principle, the paradoxical problem was that he was God, he had presented himself to them and while *He* could be an atheist, they really could not be, given the present evidence. They just couldn't deal with it. An atheist facing God is not a pretty sight. One even clamped his hands over his ears, yelling "I can't hear you, I can't hear you" over and over.

Then there was God's proclamation to the passersby that there was new evidence, scientific evidence, that there was most certainly *no God of any kind*. It is just plain materialism like the hard science guys have been saying all along. People couldn't deal with that one any more than the atheists could deal with there being a God. They didn't care what the new study said, they believed. They believed in Heaven, in Hell, in God, and that was that. God couldn't change their mind with new facts, the only facts they really cared about were the facts they believed in.

I was really starting to see the dimensions of the challenge that God had on His hands.

Suddenly God grabbed me and hustled me into a lingerie store where he began busily going through the racks of scanty panties. I thought he might have lost his mind. I wonder what that would be like if the Mind of God became deranged. Profound weather changes? Endless and meaningless war? Desperate lives scarred by poverty? Greed without hope of divine redemption? Human discourse reduced to discussions about Britney Speer's custody battles and Lindsey Lohan's rehab? We seemed to already be there, in the vortex of a God gone mad.

But God assured me he was fine. He had pulled me into the underwear store just because he was ducking the believerazzi. And as I looked out through the store window I saw them stagger by, the gaunt and dazed look of zombie believers, like an outtake from a George Romero film. I imagined a new version, *Night of the Living Believers*, when the radiation from a fallen space probe wakes the dead consumers exhausted from a life of Costco and Target shopping. The believer zombies begin looking for meaning, for purpose, for God. They notice us in the lingerie store, and begin to bang on the windows and glass door as we bar their entrance. Hungry for belief, they press against the glass, spittle falling from their lips, empty eyes looking straight at God.

The lingerie saleswoman clings to me in fright, her

world of Brazilian-cuts, V-strings and thongs crushed by the attack of the believer zombies. I know I will protect her to the end, fighting off any believer, deconstructing any belief, so that she and I will find the ecstasy we know is possible in the flow of eros. The believer zombies cannot speak, they only emit shrieks and groans as they pound on the glass. If they can find something to believe in then they will survive, the existentialist undead, the inhabitants of the borderline between nihilism and the salvation of surety, next stop *The Belief Zone*. I had entered the true nightmare of a mixed metaphor, or was that a muddled allusion.

I suddenly snapped out of it. There were no zombies, it was just a daydream gone bad, a waking nightmare, except of course that hot lingerie saleswoman, she was probably bad, but she was no bad dream. And to her, if you are out there, please get in touch, just don't contact me through my editor, she gets terribly jealous.

The believerazzi were passing by without even a glance into the lingerie store—after all, nothing they could believe in would be in such a place. These were not the ghoul believers of my dreams. They had none of the one-pointed ferocity or the otherworldly guttural sounds of believer zombies. These were real believers, my eyes were wide open. This was no fantasy. They spoke in full, intelligent and modulated sentences to each other, fervent but not out of control. They were ready to believe, but they weren't about to believe too much or too long. They were drive-by believers, sound bite believers, 15-seconds-of-belief believers. Their God would be convenient, contemporary, well marketed and undemanding.

In a way, the believerazzi just wanted a snapshot, a glimpse, a sample, nothing too heavy, definitely low-calorie. They wanted a God they could download to their iPod, text message to their friends and add as another friend on their MySpace page. The older ones would use email and talk on their cell phones, feeling sufficiently hip. They were fairly content just running back and forth, looking. That was safe enough, just looking, thank you. Finding God, or stopping the search, those were disturbing possibilities.

For God, it seemed to me, the believerazzi were a nuisance, not a real threat. It was unlikely they would see Him, let alone believe in Him. They were mainstream believers after all, not extremists. This was no jihad or crusade, just the lite diversion from the emptiness of contemporary materialism with as little effort as possible. The modern believer would never in a million eons deal with the fact that God was an atheist, that His essential communication seemed to be to demonstrate the foibles of all belief and His embrace was a one-way ticket to the unknown. They just wouldn't be interested, too intense, let's see what's on cable. In other words, God could safely leave the lingerie shop.

They wanted a God they could download to their iPod.

It is odd to admit that lingerie would trigger child-hood memories, but for me, it does because it seems that my childhood revolved around two unusual women. I actually have no memory of childhood, but with the help of a skilled and compassionate therapist, I recon-structed those early years. Consider my writing and you will understand that its origins are deeper than the experiences of this one body-mind, and perhaps that will compel you to accept what I have to tell you. Franz Kafka impregnated Alice B. Toklas in a chance encounter in Berlin in 1923 after a night of heavy drinking and cannabis smoking, and, I, Nosirrah, am the result of that undocumented tryst. This weird

occurrence, when Toklas was 46 and just a year before Kafka died of self-starvation, was never revealed
to Gertrude Stein, who thought Toklas was just eating too many brownies. This resulted in a childhood
where Nosirrah was literally and figuratively hidden
in plain sight in the Paris apartment, never spoken of,
never spoken to, and may have resulted in the deep
questioning of his very existence. I am Nosirrah, I
am that child, now old, but not as old as it would seem
doing the math, for I have also found some secrets of
staying young.

One of those secrets, which I will share with you,
is do not under any circumstances believe in the story of your life, do not believe the confirmations of a
compassionate therapist as she helps you rebuild your
past. As the stories are told and confirmed, over and
over, you will come to remember them as if they actually occurred. Nothing occurs. Everything is story,
everything is constructed. The past only exists as you
build it, and its burden is only the one that you take on
by your own creation.

Youth lies in that realization, in the eternal present, in the freedom from all that is known. My liberation was to realize that Franz Kafka, the depressive,
anxiety ridden writer, and Alice B. Toklas, inventor of
memoir cookbooks, were never my parents. I wasn't
made invisible by Gertrude Stein's anger and Alice's
complicity. I was not scarred by Kafka's death playing out the real version of "A Hunger Artist." Even

my therapist wasn't really a therapist in the classical sense, while she did charge by the hour, she was really

Alice B. Toklas, inventor of memoir cookbooks

a kind of escort of the body and the soul, and we were usually done within a premature five minutes. She did seem to listen compassionately as she got dressed, but only until she got paid, and then she left quickly, the door closing behind her with a slam. But when one door closes, another opens. I was free from my childhood, I was even free from my therapist, there is no Nosirrah, so there is no childhood to remember.

Franz Kafka, the depressive writer

Yet Stein wrote *The Autobiography of Alice B. Toklas* as a stand-in for another's life. Was I like that, a ghostly voice of another speaking through my form, my free will not really mine, my soul just an invention, my purpose given to me but not of me? Are these words that I feel entering the universe through my hand just the illusion of creativity? Am I just the created, and the meaning of my existence is that it is not, and this "not" is known to all but to me? Am I just a character in a world of words and concepts, a book *about* me but not *by* me? And you, the reader, are you also just a character written by another's hand, sure of your purpose, but somewhere experiencing the nagging sense that you are not. Perhaps you are also a contrivance, an invented reader of an invented author of an invented book without any substance at all other than that the whole construction keeps constructing.

Gertrude Stein as a stand-in

This cannot be. I am, therefore you are, dear reader. Nosirrah exists, and so must you, I think. I may not be the child of Toklas and Kafka, but I am the child of someone. They are the child of someone and on back in time to the first of us. This long chain of becoming is what I am. I am not the created, I am the creative, I am the creator.

But if so, why was God, the creator, standing there having a good laugh? God was right, God is, I am not, and I could feel the meaning and purpose drain out like a corpse being readied for embalming.

There is the shock of realization when I see my contrived identity and the utter meaninglessness of my hollow, fictional life, a kind of nom de plume of the soul. I can see myself as a ghostly doppelganger, a reflection without origin. But there is something of an indescribable dimension when I see that realization of my empty story, when I look from the unseen hand that writes the writer, who writes these words. God is, I am not, yet "I am not" walks and talks as if I am, and God is not. It is a hellish existence, a place of immense suffering, which has no substance whatsoever, no hell, no suffering, a paradox without resolution.

Which was why God was laughing, this is what He had been trying to get across to me all along. To drive home his point, he took me on a journey that landed me directly in Hell and it was truly Hellish, it was a brutal realm of pain and dementia, an unrelenting attack on any sense of goodness or sanity with absolutely no escape. Hell was my mind, it was Nosirrah. Then, like God was simply flipping a cosmic switch, we went to Heaven, which looked exactly like Hell, except Nosirrah was fictional, Hell was fictional, Heaven itself was fictional, God was fictional, there was nothing but the stream of manifestation leaving nothing behind and having nothing ahead.

This was not a dream, although it may sound like it as I attempt to describe the journey through the realms of Heaven and Hell.

I do dream. I have a recurring dream in which my day doesn't end, the dreary pursuits of the mundane life continue without cessation. In this dream there are no dreams, there is just the pulsating anxiety of the grasping survival of the waking world that goes on forever. It is a nightmare of course, and I eventually wake up so that I can get back to work, so that, exhausted, I can sleep one more night and dream that I don't dream and only work to survive. That is the Hell that God showed me, and the Heaven was the inconceivable joy of knowing that the world of survival, of struggle, was itself the dream, and that the recurring dream was the realization that I was awake to the dream.

Snap out of it Nosirrah! What has become of you, are you losing your mind? Next you will be talking about yourself in the third person and imagining you are talking to God! I had to pull myself together. Perhaps I was fictional, but I still had to function, and

God was still standing there patiently waiting for me, and even if it wasn't really God, just some allegorical prose vehicle, I couldn't really know the full implications of that anyway.

Perhaps this was the synthesis I was searching for, I couldn't know anyway, and the actual and the imagined could simply merge into one stream of consciousness even if that stream was itself imagined. But imagined by what? What is the source?

If this were a comic movie, and perhaps it is, this is where they would cue the Hari Krishnas to walk through the scene chanting, drumming, spaced out on the endless mantra, Hari Krishna, Hari Krishna, Hari Hari, Hari Rama and on and on. Krishna is the source, devotion is the path and shaved heads with goofy grins is the manifestation. It is a simple world. But in this movie, the Hari Krishnas give God a free pamphlet and walk on. In this movie, all the devotees of all the cults encounter God, give Him pamphlets and walk on. None can see God. None of them. There is an endless stream of believers handing God pamphlets about their beliefs. God takes each one and carefully places each and every one in the recycling bin. We can all rest easy, God recycles.

What God doesn't ever get is a pamphlet on the source of the comic movie, because the movie cannot see itself. The movie can show the cameras filming the movie, the director directing, the sound stage, the cables running everywhere with the gaffers and the grips scurrying about. It can wink at the viewer and let the audience in on the big joke, it is just a movie, but it can never show the camera that is showing the camera and it can never show the viewer watching the movie. The movie can't see its own blind spot. The movie can know it is a movie, but the movie cannot be conscious of anything more than that.

It is the zombie question all over again, not the believer zombies but the philosopher's zombie. If we created a zombie that had all the thoughts and feelings that we have, but was created like a machine is created, would it be conscious? This is the hard question in philosophy and in brain research, what is it that creates consciousness, does consciousness even exist or is it just an epiphenomenon of the brain function, a thought of a thought. No one seems to know the answer. Scientists agree on so much and yet they cannot agree on this most basic of qualities in life, not even whether it exists or not, let alone what it is.

This was what I wanted to confront God with, my essential question, could I be conscious, not just conscious of my self, not just conscious that I was a structure of thought, feeling and belief, but could I be conscious of consciousness itself? Could I be just consciousness, pure being, awareness residing in its own quality?

Apparently the last person who asked God about this was a guy named Ramana Maharshi, whose essential inquiry revolved around the question "Who am I?" something like an early twentieth century version of "Got milk?" Even though his wardrobe was limited to a loincloth, at least he didn't have to wear a milk mustache in magazine ads. Whatever he was, he has now become an icon in the spiritual world.

Ramana was somewhat of a dreamy boy and a poor student who left school at a young age, he was known as a good sleeper under almost any circumstance, and he was, in modern terminology, somewhat depersonalized. He took up residence in a cave on a South Indian mountain called Arunachala and sat for some years without saying a word. Soon he was a hit. Finally, he began speaking and to all the seekers who visited, he suggested they ask "Who am I?"

In the beginning of the twentieth century, the spiritual sensibility made the mystic realms fashionable, and Ramana was just one answer away from making a top spiritual fashion statement. "Who am I?" indeed. This question baffled all comers, and soon his reputation was established as one of the greatest sages of all times. Ignored was the fact that he was in love with a mountain that was basically a rocky hill, had a special relationship with a cow and was convinced that his mother had become enlightened after she finally gave up on convincing him to leave his cave. He still slept well.

Little known is the intervention by God, who showed up one day, passing through on His way to see Aurobindo in Pondicherry, and had a quick visit with

Ramana. It was not recorded by the scribes who were taking down anything and everything that Ramana said, but this is what God told me went down.

Ramana: "Who am I?"

God: "You're Ramana."

Ramana: "That's all?"

God: "That's all. Oh, one more thing."

Ramana: "What else?"

God: "You might consider not asking so many questions, putting on some clothes, and getting a life."

Ramana: "Who are you?"

God: "I'm God."

Ramana: "Why should I believe you?"

God: "Well, don't believe, just perceive, as I always say. I am not into belief, so probably you shouldn't believe Me or anything else. But, look, the way you're headed you're going to be a major brand in the years to come. It's hard to imagine that a skinny guy in a loincloth with big eyes could be right up there with Che Guevara in the t-shirt market, but you have the potential to be big. That's the good news. Bad news is that you will be dead and won't be able to hire attorneys to get control of your image."

Ramana: "What should I do?"

God: "First, stop asking questions, you'll feel better in general. But, you're kind of stuck because people are projecting so much onto your emaciated form, and believe me, I know a lot about projection. You could have a scandal, but that's been done before, and you'll only lose half your followers, the other half will explain it away as crazy wisdom or the play of the universe or some other nonsense. You could deny your insight in your talks, but then people will just think you're being super humble and even more enlightened. You could run away in the middle of the night, but your followers would make it into an ascension. You could get married and get a job, but let's face it, you're a bit of a space case, you're probably not employable."

God continued, "Let me tell you a parable. A mouse and a snake collided in the forest one day and while they were inclined to fight over their smashup, they discovered that they were both blind from birth and so, forgiving each other, became interested in discovering who they were, never having seen themselves. So the snake wrapped himself around the mouse, describing the little feet, the furry covering and the pointy face, and exclaiming, "You must be a mouse!" The mouse, feeling the snake said, "You've got slimy skin, you've got a long scaly body with beady eyes and a flickering forked tongue, I know, you must be a guru!"

Ramana: "Is that funny?"

God: "OK, that wasn't very funny. It was actually a lawyer joke. You know, the snake is a lawyer. But you get the point, I think. Ramana, you're going to get stuck being a guru, not just a guru, but a guru of gurus. Spiritual seekers are going to come here, sit in front of you, and since you aren't saying much, they're going to fill in the space with what suits them. They're going to hear you tell them they are enlightened. They're going to believe that enlightenment is just that easy, and then tell their students that each and every student is enlightened. Soon the world is going to be crawling with people who think they're enlightened. This is worse than tragic, it's absurd. Ramana, you will have to say something to the world, but say nothing at the same time."

Ramana: "Who am I?"

God: "I guess that will have to do it."

In the end Ramana may have tuned into pure consciousness, he may or may not have gotten what God had to say, lots of people prop up his picture behind their chairs when they give their enlightenment talks. But, it isn't that easy to find a Ramana t-shirt. If you look carefully at some of the old pictures of Ramana, you will see on occasion he does wear a t-shirt himself, and written on it is, "I'm enlightened, and all I got was this lousy t-shirt." Most of us won't even get that, because really we're not looking very carefully at all. God, like the great magician he is, does his best to redirect our attention, but like he says, we are always looking the wrong way. Sometimes God has to confuse us to keep us from the foolishness of our certainty.

Ramana Maharshi, spiritual icon

But back to the fundamental question of our consciousness, could I be consciousness itself, without ending up on t-shirts? What could that possibly look like? As I reflected on this question I recalled something I didn't want to remember. We all have a time of our life we would like to forget, a dark period, a period of disorganization, and for me it was my time at Harvard. I would like to tell you how I studied there, and of course, it may be evident from my brilliance that this would be the case, but I will be quite candid with you, I never studied at Harvard, I was being studied. It was a difficult time, the worst of times really, and yet it was the time of greatest change, a spiritual metamorphosis, where the caterpillar I was changed entirely by becoming a meal for a crow, metaphorically speaking.

At that time in my life, I had assumed that I was residing in pure consciousness, or simply put, that I was enlightened, a story I have already told in great detail in my semi-autobiographical science fiction romance memoir novella *Practical Obsession*. It was so clear to me that I had transcended, yet this was the enlightenment of the caterpillar, only a relative breakthrough as I was about to discover.

I thought that Harvard Medical School of all places would be the place to confirm the radiant unity that I was experiencing. Perhaps they would want to do some CAT scans and see what one such as I was made of, a breakthrough study of the undivided mind.

The doctors seemed fascinated with my description of the unitary world and the flow of my consciousness through all of reality. I laid out how all of those who appeared to be separate where in fact me. I told the doctor that he may think of himself as a solid entity, but could he not know with certainty he was. He began muttering something about "Capgras delusion." But, it was when I explained to him that even the stuffed animal on his shelf had a form of consciousness that he really got excited, uttering "Ah, delusional companions." He hit one of his intercom buttons and soon I was whisked off for the scans I had known they would want, but for some reason they insisted on sedating me with a rather large syringe of Thorazine.

Delusional misidentification syndrome was what they called it. I called it enlightenment. I was one with all beings and they were convinced I had a serious brain disorder.

I had never heard of the things they were talking about, intermetamorphosis and clonal pluralization. Apparently these were psychiatric conditions where people thought their friends and family had been swapped out with identical but alien beings, and that they themselves had multiple identical clones scattered about. But, for me these were not thoughts, these were perceptions. These were the elements of my fundamental realization. It was difficult explaining this to the doctors because they kept switching themselves out for identical doctors who were entirely new each moment, and there I was, cloned over and over, ever present. They upped the Thorazine levels to the maximum.

If you have had any medical training, you might know that Thorazine can have a lot of side effects, including abnormal secretion of milk, abnormalities in movement and posture, agitation, anemia, asthma, blood disorders, breast development in males, chewing movements, constipation, difficulty breathing, difficulty swallowing, dizziness, drooling, drowsiness, dry mouth, ejaculation problems, eye problems causing fixed gaze, fainting, fever, flu-like symptoms, fluid accumulation and swelling, headache, heart attack, high or low blood sugar, hives, inability to urinate, inability to move or talk, increase of appetite, infections, insomnia, intestinal blockage, involuntary movements of arms and legs, tongue, face, mouth, or jaw, irregular blood pressure, pulse, and heartbeat, jitteriness, lockjaw, mask-like face, muscle stiffness and rigidity, narrow or dilated pupils, nasal congestion, nausea, pain and stiffness in the neck, persistent, painful erections, pill-rolling motion, protruding tongue, puckering of the mouth, puffing of the cheeks, rapid heartbeat, red or purple spots on the skin, rigid arms, feet, head, and muscles (including the back), seizures, sensitivity to light, severe allergic reactions, shuffling walk, skin inflammation and peeling, sore throat, spasms in jaw, face, tongue, neck, mouth, and feet, sweating, swelling of the throat, tremors, twitching in the body, twisted neck, visual problems, yellowed skin and whites of eyes.

Usually when some of these symptoms show up, an alert doctor will change the medication. In my case, *all* of the side effects showed up, all at once.

I had asked for total transformation in my life, and now it had arrived in an unexpected way and an unimagined form. He who had entered the Harvard Medical Center as an enlightened man had transformed into something entirely new and unrelated to the past form, possibly unrelated to the human form. Now, where I had vanished, Nosirrah emerged, albeit with peeling skin and a painful erection, unable to speak or move, among other disconcerting troubles, but in a state of transcendent bliss that would make the manufacturers of Thorazine proud.

The doctor meanwhile was having an entirely different experience. He was an intern in the final year of his high pressured academic career with just the psych ward rotation left to go, whose dream was to become a successful dermatologist and whose entire life since preschool had been made up of expertly acing multiple choice tests.

He looked at the emergent Nosirrah, with my yellow eyes, tongue protruding, male breasts secreting milk, jittery tremoring, not to mention the painful erection which must have been particularly frightening to a man with such a little weenie, and the good doctor had to make a quick decision to the real life test question, either a) an alien being had been transported to the psych ward, b) the doctor was actually asleep and having a bad dream, c) the doctor himself had gone mad and was having a psychotic break, or d) all of the above. Apparently the correct answer was d) all of the above, and the doctor ran screaming from the examination room while injecting himself with my remaining Thorazine dosage.

I was a free man on every possible level and as the Thorazine wore off and I could begin moving again, I strolled out of the ward, out of the hospital, and into the cool breeze of a new day. I may have been a clone of myself, but that clone was fully alive if only just for this moment.

Of course, as I walked from the hospital, it occurred to me that I had no idea what to do with my new post-spiritual life. I remembered in Zen it is taught that first you chop wood, then you get enlightened, and then you chop wood again. I was a little afraid I would cut off my leg if I tried that one, but it is also possible I didn't understand the metaphor. I mean, who chops wood these days?

What would Al Gore do? He had to face a post-political life after he won the presidential election in 2000. He was a lame duck before he was even a duck. He broke the record of thirty-one days held by William Henry Harrison for the shortest presidential term, and Al didn't even have to die suddenly of pneumonia. He was President-elect, and then he was not. It was a new kind of election, in a new kind of political system, a magical democracy. Now you see it, now you don't.

When Al walked out into the fresh morning air the next day, contemplating his post-political life, did he envision making a documentary on global warming that would get him the Oscar and the Nobel Peace Prize while what's his name went down in history as the absolute worst president of all time, including all planets, all possible alternative universes, and all dimensions of reality—just the absolute zero of all worsts? Al could not have known these things, all he could do was face the empty space that was the life he had known, and the infinite possibility of what was about to occur. He could not have known that once he collected the Oscar and the Nobel Peace Prize, he would trade them in for a seat on the board of one of the largest venture capital firms in the world where he could be doing good by doing well, extremely well. All Gandhi got to do was homespun cotton, imagine, if he had joined the board of Monsanto, he might have guided them away from genetically modified cotton in India, taking the conglomerate green and collecting handsome stock options. But that was back in the day, this is a different time, an era when heroes are immensely wealthy and …well that's enough, just immensely wealthy.

Maybe this was a clue for me, I would emulate Al

Gore. I would call my movie *An Inconvenient Relative Truth*, in which I would point out that all of reality is a construction of the mind. I would relentlessly travel, showing my charts and graphs. I would turn down the Oscar and the Peace Prize as created realities, and in the notoriety that followed, take my place on the board of the World Bank where I would puncture the myth of capitalism by pointing out that it is basically all paper. Press release: All debts are hereby forgiven from car loans, student loans and mortgages all the way to the national debt of all nations. I would run up my credit card before the announcement, and, by the way, if you see Nosirrah appointed to the board of the World Bank, you should, too.

But I am not really Peace Prize material, and I don't really like charts and graphs. They remind me of my hospitalizations. Come to think of it, psychology is what I know best, I have had enough of it applied to me over the years. I could launch myself as Dr. Nos with a daytime television program where I bring on really unhappy people and assertively show them what morons they are for arguing with each other, keeping messy houses, having bratty kids and not recognizing the unitary nature of the universe. It is not important that their lives are fundamentally disordered, shallow and materialistic. They only have to realize that they are simply manifestations of the flow of conscious-ness itself—duh! *Wake up, people, you are just empty phe-nomenon. You are not, because the universe is! We'll be right back after the break—don't go away!*

As Dr. Nos, I would write best-selling books that my editor wouldn't dare alter, like *How to Be Nothing Without Being a Nobody*, in which I help the reader see that their life is as non-existent as their checking account balance. Don't try to fix your neurotic mind and your pathetic marriage—it doesn't exist, just thought bubbles in the moment, vaporous emptiness in the guise of a self.

That seems boring though, maybe it is better to go with a VH1-like reality show in which twenty lovely ladies vie to be a permanent part of Nosirrah's life. *The Noz of Love* will have uncensored cam shots of me trying to decide which of the ladies will be eliminated as I make the emotionally excruciating choices to finally decide which five will remain as my wives. Or six if it really gets difficult towards the end, because I don't want to hurt anyone's feelings, even though feelings are as empty as thoughts.

But, this is all too old media, passé. The youth aren't watching cable anymore. I am going to have to move the platform to the web. Let the users generate the content. Democratize the production. It is the wisdom of crowds of 17-year-olds. I will call it UTurnTube™ and it will be an easy interface in which millions of young users upload real-time video cam images of themselves uploading to UTurnTube, and they can then download the uploads of themselves, playing it back instantly. Imagine millions of young people entranced at images playing in real time of themselves in front of their computers staring back at them while they sit at their computer. It is really a killer app and the only question is how to monetize it. Maybe run Google click-through ads that advertise the user's name, and when the user clicks on it, it brings them automatically back to their own UTurn-Tube site while generating a little revenue for the clever inventor. The beauty of the concept is that it is scalable and it can travel to the emerging mobile web platform—one can imagine the entire world population gazing at real time images on iPhones of themselves moving through their own lives. With coming miniaturization, this could simply be implanted in the corneas, or better in the synapses with tiny nanobots reflecting to us our life just a split second after it occurs.

God was clearing His throat, and since God doesn't really have throat phlegm it could only mean that He wanted to interrupt my thought stream to inject something relatively sane. It turns out that our brain is already designed as a UTurnTube platform and God holds the patent. We're already watching our lives a fraction of a second after it happens. Even the brain scientists seem to be on board for this one. We act, we cognate, we reorganize the cognition temporally so that it seems like we created the action from the cognition.

We have a sense of free will, and a sense that it

comes from our thinking mind, and can happily go about our business. That clever God set it up that way so our little pea brains wouldn't get confused by understanding that we were simply acting without anything prior other than the prior actions all the way back to the beginning of time. The best technologies are the ones that run silently in the background, working flawlessly and without any operator needed. God imbedded some pretty dandy technology in us and then in the coup de grace, let us believe that we are doing it. We feel safe that way, just like we do when we go through airport screening. Even though I know I am not going to blow up a plane, I feel so much safer after being frisked and having my toothpaste taken away, and I am sure you do, too. I feel safer thinking that I am running my life, that I have free will, and that I am the master of my actions. I am sure you do, too.

That was the real original sin—feeling safe by making up a nice story. According to God, it was a little different in the Garden than some of the accounts, or as He put it, they all got it backwards. Mostly the religionists have mankind in a state of ignorant bliss and then in an act of disobedience to God, and tempted by the serpent, the first couple taste the fruit of knowledge and lose their innocence, their long-term lease on the Garden and the scourge of tan lines began. This is a story, the original story, and that is exactly the issue. There isn't any original sin, the so-called sin is a story, and the only real loss of innocence is the human preoccupation with confabulation. We will tell any tale to make the world make sense to us. We are addicted to narrative with the vaguest of logical sequencing, but as long as we have a story we feel safe. Naked people eating an apple in a heavenly garden with a devilish snake—now that is the reason that I better get to my place of religious worship, for I have been born into sin. It is not a great story, it doesn't really hold up that well over the centuries, although it must have been mightily impressive in the early years before education became widespread. But, flawed as it might be, it is a story.

The story is not *about* the fall of man, it *is* the fall of man. It establishes us firmly in the past by describing what we are experiencing solely in terms of the past. We can't escape from the past. We can't discover anything new. We are stuck in the loop of our own story. This is the original estrangement, not from God, but from what is actually going on in life.

How do we handle that disconnect? We simply include it in our story. The disconnect from the actual flow of life is sin, and the connection to the lifestream, well, let's just call that God. Obedience to God will wash away our sin. Connection will cure our disconnection. It doesn't get anymore tautological than that.

Let's review. It's the Stone Age, and we have no idea what is going on in life other than it certainly is going. We don't feel that great because we don't have any control—floods wash away our villages, lightening strikes our goats and mysterious diseases wipe out our offspring. We look for causation, but not having the technology to get to the bottom of the mystery, we say God did it because we are bad. We will be good, if we can figure out what it is God wants. Enter the religionists who explain where we went wrong and how we can get right with God. If we are right with God, the floods won't come and therefore, logically, if the floods come, we are not right with God. Periodically the floods come, lightening strikes our goats, and mysterious diseases continue to wipe out our offspring. The religionists prosper, the story becomes imbedded in the human psyche and each of us continues to build narratives that explain to ourselves how we can be safe in a world that is going quite fast. Most of us are pretty sure there is a God so we don't have to get into the deeper mysteries of life, that's His department. We know that we are missing something, and it is probably because of that snake and the apple. We know that our religion has promised to take care of that if we follow the rules. This frees us up to stay focused on our personal stories: my wife doesn't love me, I'm not respected at work, I don't like that guy across the street who cuts his lawn on Sunday mornings when I want to sleep in.

If there is no story then there is no religion, no personal problems, no God. There is just the cosmos flowing, and maybe not even that. Thank God we have our stories.

But then why was God telling me all of this, even Nosirrah has his limits. I have loved, I have lived, I have even died as I have described in *Practical Obsession*. But can the human being handle the flow of the cosmos without reducing it to a convenient concept? And more so, does this human being have the capacity to live in that cosmic flow which is not a thing, not of time, not of location, without meaning or causation? I felt the atomic structure of my being shifting in and out of occurrence, swapping electrons, merging with the dark matter that enveloped the positive material. Nothing moved and there was nothing. There was nothing.

God laughed, and took my hand, as I could barely walk, and led me through the doorway of a used bookstore. There we walked to the very back, to the place where in every used book store there is a pile of boxes of books that can neither be discarded nor be placed on any shelf, a literary purgatory of forgotten titles on subjects no longer in the cultural lexicon, yet each book still potent in and of itself.

God reached into the box on top and pulled out a book, handing it to me, and as I read the cover, the shock was too much for my frail nervous system, and I crumpled to the floor like a tasered drunk. It was not the title that smashed into me, a title I did not recognize in any event, an odd almost mocking title, *Nothing from Nothing*. Rather it was the author of this strange book, that author being me, Nosirrah. I had written a book that I could not even recall.

The shock was too much for my frail nervous system.

There was one more blank spot in my life filling in, and this book was it. I was flooded with eidetic rec-ollections of a different time and place, the aroma of coffee brewed strong, the shadows of morning light playing on the peeling walls, as I sat at my typewriter forcing my fingers to write the words that I couldn't bear to read. It was my book, a book I had written, a book still alive although long out of print and with no shelf that could hold it. *Nothing from Nothing* was a book that had consumed me even as I wrote it so many years before, a book that had cost me everything in my life and had given me naught.

I had tried to destroy that book when it was still just a manuscript, but my editor had a copy, and she published it despite my pleas. That book shattered our love, and left us with nothing. I tried to buy up the copies, to obliterate the words that had been written, but it was too late. I could only destroy myself, and not even that could be accomplished because I knew that I was already nothing. And, then, in those long gone days, nothingness enveloped me, there was no book, there was no world, there was just the cosmos. And then there was nothing. Nothing from nothing.

Then there was something. This. Now. I threw down the book and staggered from the book store, God right along side humming the "Battle Hymn of the Republic," which I supposed was a sardonic commentary on the ridiculous struggles of the human being to face their own meaninglessness. No, he assured me, no derision intended, that was just my story, he simply liked those old rollicking hymns. He also likes blues and indie rock. And He wanted to point out to me that I was alive and well even though I was nothing. I didn't have to struggle with facing my own meaninglessness because if my life was meaningless then it would be really a waste of energy to struggle. I got the logic of what He was saying, and I did find it interesting that nothing wasn't as bad as I remembered it. In fact, it was actually rather relaxing.

I didn't need to struggle. I didn't need to have an explanation. I was the expression of the universe. I was the flow of consciousness itself. But this left me, like the book that I am now writing and that you are now reading, without a plot, without a protagonist, without any tension to resolve.

Except that there is one small tension and that is that the now in which I am writing this is different from the now that you are reading it, isn't it? If there are two nows then there must be something that connects them, and this is time, and then I can have an action, I can do something, I can even salvage this novel by creating something interesting to the reader, I will sell again, I will be wanted as a author again and then I won't have to argue with that case worker every month about my food stamps.

If you are reading this, then you are in another universe looking in to this one. You are giving me the gift of time, so that I can act, so that I can do, you are creating me even as I create these words that you will read. You, my dear reader, are my God, because you create me by reading these words. You create the God that I walk through this tale with, the God who is not, the God who is me, but now we can see that God in actuality is you. You can destroy just as easily as you create. You destroy by closing this book. Do it. Destroy. Now open the book and create. You are reading this, creating this, destroying this, as you please. I worship you by writing, but I also hate you for making me your slave, dependent on you for my very existence. I see your weakness. You are a god who believes in yourself, you have not found your atheism. The God of my book cannot be destroyed, because He does not exist. But you can be destroyed very easily, even from this moment that I write no matter how far it is to the moment you read this. I will just stop writing and you and I will cease to be.

You see, it is madness to believe. It is madness to believe in yourself, to believe in God, to believe in yourself as God. And it is madness to believe in nothing at all. It is madness to believe, just to believe.

But the real insanity is to believe that this moment that I write is different than the moment you read, that the writer is separate from the reader, that the God that I create is different than the God that you create. Differentiation is madness, it creates false structures of time and place where there are none.

Confabulation is sanity. If I need a plot in my life, I can just make one up, just like I can do in this novel. We know the plot is a fabrication, but that is what a novel is and that is what a life is.

Here is the plot. A man accidentally runs into God. Time and space collapse when God reveals that He doesn't believe in Himself. The man sees the nature of reality and beyond in a series of powerful vignettes that do happen in time and space, but are only loosely related by the idea that the man is walking around a city with God. The man realizes that he is God, and that he doesn't exist. Paradoxically, he lives happily ever after, primarily because I want to sell the film rights to this book and test audiences always go for a happy ending. I want Jack Nicholson to play me, or maybe Tommie Lee Jones. I want a really hot young actress like Scarlett Johansson to play my love interest, which I will have to write into the screenplay if I don't get around to it in this book. (I am making a note to myself to remember to do that, because I really want to meet Scarlett or whoever is young and hot when the film goes into production, so look for a juicy female to show up later in the novel unless I forget). I want my editor to be played by some old, brooding actress, a faded beauty who has become embittered and nasty, maybe Faye Dunaway. She can also play the part of the unpleasant Goddess that devours me so people will get the connection to my editor since that probably isn't so clear in my writing. God will have to be played off camera or maybe by an old character actor that everybody has forgotten and who has been drinking heavily for years so there is a lot of quality in his voice.

During the film shooting, I will take up with Scarlett, she being smitten with the wit and talent of Nosirrah the screenwriter. We will hop the globe from Cannes to Cancun, settling only occasionally in our Malibu compound or our New York loft. We will have little Scarletta and Nosirrah, Jr. in between my screenwriting meaningful blockbusters, and Scarlett being Scarlett in whatever movies she deems worthy of her incredible talent and looks. I will grow younger in this new successful lifestyle, not just because I will have the funds to eat regularly, but I will also have a personal trainer and some repair work on my time-ravaged face. I will forget the troubles of the past, and drink a glass of bubbly to the future that will always look bright, and to the hundreds of new friends that success has brought. I will get a record breaking advance on the updated reissue of my autobiography, *Practical Obsession*.

Scarlett will probably be lazy with her workouts though, and having children will not be good for her figure. I will begin to notice the hysteria in that little laugh that she does when she is feeling at all insecure. Her depressions will grow longer and more unbearable for me, and when her constant demands on my attention begin to affect my writing, I will be forced to leave her for a newer and younger starlet.

The tabloids will have a field day, of course, and the paparazzi will hound us while the divorce is played out in the press. She will get it all, the children, the money, even my typewriter because she will muster up her considerable theatrical talents and convince the judge and the public that I am a madman, that I am just a mediocre writer, that my award-winning screenplays were ghostwritten by my editor. The public will hate me, the judge will rule against me, Random House will cancel my autobiography, the newer and younger starlet will leave me, my screenplay royalties will be assigned to my editor and I will never see my children again. A broken man, I will have to wait decades to get a brief spot on *Entertainment Tonight*, in a "where are they now" feature, and actually the show will be on Scarlett—my presence will be limited to my right ear as the camera lingers on her as it always does. Meanwhile, Scarlett will get herself back in shape and become the new old Faye Dunaway, faded beauty, yes, but you would still love to have a night with her. Scarlett, why did we let this happen to us?

I will be left to write unpublishable tomes about meeting God. I will be left with my editor pestering me, as she is these days, to complete this novella. She acts as if her irritating messages will somehow stimulate more words to come from these aching hands, as if she can wring more from this mind that has already traveled too far into the unknown realms of divine madness. But she will get her book. She knows very well how to push me, even past the limits of my health and sanity. I will write on, but I will simply write what comes. I am the John Cage of writers. Cage made sounds and called it music, I make letters and call them words, call them sentences, call them books.

No one knows what to do with what I write. They are afraid to ignore my work—it may be declared genius in another generation. They are afraid to read it—they fear that they might join the fragmenting reality that I inhabit, never to return to the known. They will buy a few thousand copies to be left on coffee tables, bookshelves or used to prop open windows as insurance against the possible discovery of my brilliance. Finally, out of print, what few copies remain will end up misshelved in a dusty second-hand book store, seemingly forgotten, but still potent, still dangerous, still unknown.

The one who picks up that used and discarded copy, who touches its scratched cover and bent pages, who reads it despite the underlining and moronic notes left in the margins by the first handful of owners, that is the one for whom this book is written. It is not likely that it is written for you, you are likely just the agent to pass the book on, if you don't destroy it first. If you are the one for whom this book is written, then you cannot stop reading these lines. You know that is your destiny even as you read these words, and you know intuitively that these are the words that come next, they are the only words that could have been written next and they are the only words that will ever be written next. These words are what is.

If you are the one for whom this book is written, then you also know that this book could not be written for you, because you are not. Yet, this book was written for you, and only you. You have not escaped the significance of this encounter although you might like to. Thousands upon thousands of copies had to be printed, distributed, sold, resold again and again, discarded, lost or destroyed just to get this one copy into your hands. Can your hands hold this book? Can your eyes read it? Can you bear the intensity of it? I cannot. I must go back to the story of my meeting with God.

The problem with meeting God is that, if instead of fumbling around asking all kinds of inane questions, you ask Him to help you find the one essential inquiry, "What is the ultimate question?"—he will give you the philosophy grad student's smug reply, "That was the ultimate question, and this is the answer to it." Ha, ha. If you ask him the ultimate question yourself, "What is the meaning of life?' then he is going to give you the inscrutable, the absurd and the paradoxical, like a cosmic Zen master.

God is not trying to be coy, and certainly not Zen, although He could probably get a bestseller out of it, *The Zen of God* or something like that. He is just tickled at the question and He is answering, it is just that the answer is happening too quickly. Remember, he is timeless, and that is very, very quick. We are like the snail that got mugged by the gang of turtles and when the police ask the snail what happened the snail has to admit he has no idea because it happened too fast.

The scene of the crime

God is fast, not just here and now fast, faster than that. God is the future pulling us forward. Faster than a speeding bullet, faster than the speed of light, sorry Einstein, but it's true: God is faster than time itself.

It is a pacing issue, as Larry Byram, founder of Alignment Technologies and advisor to celebrities and Fortune 500 CEOs, would say. Some people take little bits of information at a rapid clip, they are fast paced. Others take larger chunks at a slower rate. You may notice this with some of your relationships—in some relationships you are constantly waiting for the person to catch up to what you are saying and in others you are running to keep up yourself. Snails and turtles. God is taking infinite chunks at an unfathomable speed. Even Larry can't keep up with God, but he is pretty close.

So you can imagine when the religious reporters of history tried to take notes, whether they were snails or turtles, they could only get the crib notes. Maybe for those individuals with direct contact the notes helped them relate to the ultimate rush of their meeting with God. But, for the ones who came after, who read the notes, or translated them into the next language, or met in councils to decide what to leave in, what to take out and what to add, the holy books became something else. These books became religious beliefs based on nothing more than the circular argument of their inerrancy. This is the snail's police report handed down for generations as if the account was accurate. Generations of snails later and wars are being fought over the interpretation of the translation of the account of the turtles mugging the snail, an account which no snail could possibly have written accurately because it happened too fast.

The religious followers' response to the absurdity of the situation is the rationalization that it must have been a very special snail who wrote the report-which-no-snail-could-have-written-accurately. Believe it or not. And by the way, if you don't believe it, you are going to burn in an unspecified but truly awful Hell for all of eternity and possibly be stoned, impaled or blown up to help you get there faster.

Atheist snails mock the whole belief system built around the holy books, point to the historic inaccuracies, the cultural context, the translation errors, the constant rewriting and editing. They have a good laugh, and if you have ever heard a snail laugh you know exactly what I mean, and, as an aside, you should also see a good psychiatrist to get your meds adjusted.

The atheist snails laugh at the beliefs around the mystical contact with God, but they also have no idea what actually did happen, or the potential of what could happen in such an encounter. The atheist snails are fast snails, but they are still too slow, and, as I mentioned before, God is very fast. The atheists laugh, but it is the laugh of one who does not love uncertainty. It is an anxious laugh, one that finds a relative surety in the disdain for fools, but holds no wisdom of its own, and certainly no joy. A smug atheist may see the joyous believer as a moron, but a joyous atheist is an oxymoron.

What do you get when you cross an atheist with a believer? I believe I don't know.

To not know is the end of the world, so we like to fill the void with…the end of the world. We love the notion of the end times. We have probably been speculating on the end of the world since the beginning of the world, or at least since we noticed the first eclipse and wondered if the sun was going out. We have endless competing theories of the end of the world from the wildly imaginative (but possibly true) Christian apocalyptic final battle and rapture where the righteous are lifted up into heaven to the other end of the rationality spectrum with the statistically proven, analytic projection of a global warming induced climate collapse (which is also possibly true). Now, maybe all of the end of the world scenarios are accurate and fit together like pieces of a puzzle, the picture only revealed as the last piece falls into place—like when the rapture comes and the righteous rise up to heaven, while the rest of us will be burning in a Hell world, and that would certainly qualify as global warming.

Apparently the Mayan calendar comes to an end in 2012 and not surprisingly there is an entire industry being built around various New Age 2012 end of the world scenarios, likely by the same crew that brought you the Harmonic Convergence in 1987 and the Y2K Catastrophe in 2000.

Will the world end in 2012? Will I be left behind in the rapture? As I considered these possibilities, I must say that I certainly hope I am left behind if all believers of all beliefs ascend to heaven, it might solve overpopulation, terrorism and a host of other issues that have really been bugging me. If all the believers of all the beliefs go to heaven, doesn't heaven become the hell they were trying so hard to escape as they continue their sectarian fighting? If the believers go, doesn't hell on earth become pretty mellow? Even if the believers are right, especially if they are right, I want to be left behind in 2012 anyway, as long as all the believers go to their heaven.

But since I don't have faith in the end time beliefs and I don't think anyone is going anywhere, I am floating a new book proposal tentatively titled *2013: How to Profit from the Prophets in the Coming End of the World.* Imagine the opportunities in real estate, used automobiles, jewelry, small appliances and furniture, not to mention stocks and bonds, as the believers unload their earthly possessions in anticipation of the end of the world in 2012. After midnight on December 31, 2012, you start selling it all back to them with a mark-up plus storage and handling fees. Storage could be an issue if you are trying to hold onto the possessions of six and half billion people for six to twelve months, but I am thinking I will just throw a tarp over it all and hope it doesn't rain. Like I said, I am still working out the details, and details have never been my strong point. I am more of a big picture person.

The big picture is not believing in any picture. If you don't believe, then you are always going to be a cultural contrarian. To you the world will look like a society of madness, but let's be clear that the world will not see you as the sane one. It is like the guy who is driving down the freeway and hears on the radio that there is a crazed driver going the wrong way down that very highway. The guy says to himself, "A crazed driver? It looks to me like there are hundreds of them!"

Somehow in our walk around the city, God and I had come back to the busy intersection that was the spot of our meeting and I realized in that timelessness sort of way, my time with God was running out. I had to give up on the meaning of life area and get into something practical, concrete, down-to-earth. What are we supposed to do about all of this? If God could get irritated, then this was an irritating direction to take my line of questioning. Doing is a contrived concept after all, the notion that we sit outside of ourselves, outside of life itself and through a series of independent calculations make a decision which we then step back into our life to apply. We like to think that we are the decider and that the actions that come from our decisions define the meaning of our life. God was very clear on this point, and it is really the beginning of the real end. By that I mean the beginning of the end of me, and of you, and of this book.

If you understand that you do not stand outside of your life, that you do not exist in separation from life, that you do not have any opportune distance from God, then you also understand that you do not have any action to take. There is nothing for you to do because you are being done. You are the debris field of the moving energy of life. The action results in you, you do not take any action. You are not. Energetic movement is. Life is just as it occurs.

Ah, but that is a profound understanding that you do not possess. You are certain that you exist, so you are left with the question of what to do. You believe that you are, that you decide, that you must know what to do in order to decide. This is a convenient untruth sans slide show other than the pictures and graphs of your own mind.

I believed that I was, that I must know, that I must act. I slammed myself over and over into God. What shall I do? Tell me what to do! Enough of this vast, timeless view, what about the small me that needs to decide how to live? But my slamming into God over and over was the perfect metaphor, despite the fact that such perfection is imbedded in a faltering novel. Of all the actions, the only thing I could do was to find God, to find the one thing which was beyond my belief and my concepts, to take the one action that had nothing prior to it, nothing causing it, nothing doing it. Creatio ex nihilo by the created, the paradox of nothing from nothing. Nihilo ex nihilo. Pure creation. Creatio Purusaum. Pure energy. Purusha. All that has been and all that will be, all of it Purusha, all of it sacrificed on the fires of creation.

So, if you are convinced that you must do something, do that thing. There is only one action. Find God, not the God of your beliefs, or the God of someone else's beliefs, but the God that does not exist, the God who is an atheist. Take that action. You have run out of time, so do it now.

If time still exists for you, then you will defer that one action and obscure it in a course of actions. If you cannot find that singular action, then you are left to find the actions that take you to that one action. Strip away your beliefs one by one. They can do you no good in discovering God. Discard them, each and every one of them. Never look back, never look forward and most certainly do not look in this moment, but look everyplace else that you can find. God waits for you where you do not want to venture, just beyond your beliefs.

But if you cannot see your own belief structures then you have a different discovery to make and no action will be of use to you. If you cannot find your beliefs, then you cannot discard them. Is it that they are veiled in the dream that is your life? You will find your beliefs embodied there in the dream. You believe in the job that you hold, the marriage you are committed to, the parents to whom you were born. You believe in your bank account, in the food in your refrigerator, the heat coming from your furnace that tells you that you are secure.

You cannot discard such a life even though it is built entirely upon belief, that belief is your imagined safety. You cannot free yourself from the claws of the promise that you will survive even as you are devoured by the ennui of the mundane. It is the languorous trance that keeps you safe, the delectable torpor that protects you from seeing anything at all.

There is no hope for you in the bubble-wrapped life of survival, security and safety. Despite your spiritual practices and your religious faith, you will never find your way out because you have no intention of ever doing so. And, if you find yourself in the haze without hope then you are at the point of insight, the book you hold in your hand can be put away, and you can simply see that even without any hope, even in a Kevlar life of belief, you can breath in, but you do not know if you will ever breathe out again. You can breathe out, but you do not know that you will breathe in. When you do not know, and when you breathe even in this unknowing, you are no longer slamming into God, you have met God, the God who is not there but who is the very breath that you are.

I had stopped slamming into God, I had stopped questioning, I had stopped everything but I did, for some mysterious and inexplicable reason, breathe. Time did not flow forward, only backward in that moment. All the past opened up as a view of human consciousness in all its expressions, but what was next was without time, or form, or any condition whatsoever. It was creation itself, it was entirely free, beyond me, beyond belief, and beyond the God whose eyes met mine in love without separation.

As I gazed at this being who is only movement, this stillness that is only action, this God who is not, this Other who is me, I dove, or was it fell, into the essence of this God who is me, in a dizzying, disorienting, ecstatic look from those eyes that actually see what is, and in seeing what is, see what isn't, and in seeing what isn't, see all. What those eyes of God see is that what is seen is also God, there is no separation, there is no other, there is no God. From those eyes, I saw a car that came at me, taking a hard turn on a red light, and screeching to a halt just inches from me. The driver jumped from the car, all apologies, all concern, all fear, and looked into my eyes, and saw God, God looking back and seeing himself, me looking back and seeing myself. And then we went for coffee.

Sentient Publications would like to acknowledge www.NosirrahIsNot.com for supporting this project.

Sentient Publications, LLC publishes books on cultural creativity, experimental education, transformative spirituality, holistic health, new science, ecology, and other topics, approached from an integral viewpoint. Our authors are intensely interested in exploring the nature of life from fresh perspectives, addressing life's great questions, and fostering the full expression of the human potential. Sentient Publications' books arise from the spirit of inquiry and the richness of the inherent dialogue between writer and reader.

Our Culture Tools series is designed to give social catalyzers and cultural entrepreneurs the essential information, technology, and inspiration to forge a sustainable, creative, and compassionate world.

We are very interested in hearing from our readers. To direct suggestions or comments to us, or to be added to our mailing list, please contact:

SENTIENT PUBLICATIONS, LLC

1113 Spruce Street
Boulder, CO 80302
303-443-2188
contact@sentientpublications.com
www.sentientpublications.com